Bridge Event

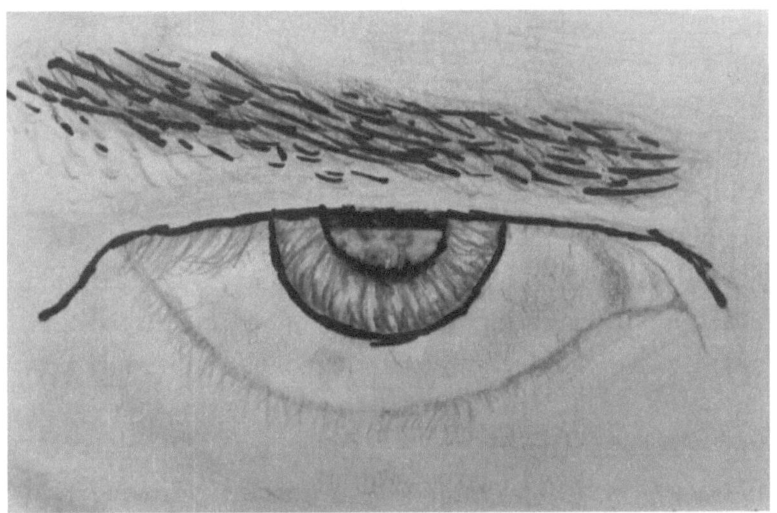

Written by Talon Abrams
Cover Art Drawn by Maria Peavey
Inside Art Drawn by Abby Abrams

ONE

Interdimensional travel. The words themselves sounded insane but this was all real. Amazingly it had only taken 6 months to create a working dimensional portal that the scientists at US Facility 12 called, The Bridge. Doctor Robert Allen was the head scientist at this facility. He worked on this project for the past half a year alongside the United States military and Central Intelligence Agency. Built deep within the forest of the Adirondack Mountains in upstate New York, far away from any population centers, there was a time that this was one of the most top secret facilities in the country. The idea for an interdimensional bridge was first thought up to try to find a way to cure the incurable pandemic that had terrorized the entire world. This mutated form of coronavirus swept the world at an amazing rate, unseen by any other disease in history. Within a year, 1 billion people worldwide had brutally died at the hands of this disease; but just like many other pandemics throughout history, one day it just mysteriously disappeared leaving life of the humans on earth to go (somewhat) back to normal; however, the search for dimensional travel continued for 2 reasons. The first, they needed to find a vaccine in case the virus ever came back. Trial after trial resulted in failure and many people died trying to contain this virus. The effects of the virus were quite brutal resulting in organs basically melted by fever, and lungs collapsed from coughing leading to convulsions. The world didn't need to see another outbreak of this virus. They were lucky that only 1 billion had died worldwide. A brutal death toll due to their lack of preparedness for a pandemic. The second reason for the continued research was to unite the broken nation. After the government had failed to assist the citizens of the United States in their time of need, there was little faith in the government. During the pandemic the government failed to assist the people of the nation with food and income, and chose instead to play politics. Protests erupted and instead of listening to the citizens of the nation, the President met the unhappy people with military action paired with secret police abductions. Even after the virus was gone, violence had erupted between citizens. Some people made rebellions against the government, other people were creating state wide feuds against other states. Violence against people of different political beliefs ran rampant, as well as racism and greed. The nation had not been this split since the American Civil War. The idea of researching this new science would be to try to get the people to align with each other once again to share in the excitement of a changed world.

Doctor Allen believed that there was nothing more important going on anywhere in the world than right here in his facility. In fact, there were no other facilities in the world working on this, and they went public with this new science just 2 weeks ago. Allen was ecstatic. His research alone could better the world and save his country. He could be given medals! Or at least the Nobel Peace Prize, he thought. That would show that he was the top researcher in the country, hell, even the world. As a top of his class graduate from MIT, he was expected to do great things with his career; and he had. He was about to change the world.

The way that the bridge worked was through a two way connection. Nothing could go through without permission from the other side, and nothing could come through without Allen's permission. The system was perfect and with the way dimensional travel worked, the other dimension would be set during the same time as our dimension, meaning that they would be just as technologically advanced as we are now. Several test runs had gone through successfully already. It started with sending a pencil. Something simple but effective at telling if it worked. The pencil was sent and 5 minutes later it returned. Whoever was on the other side of the bridge was playing Allen's little game with him. The next trial was a letter. Something simple, saying "hello". 5 minutes later a similar note returned saying, "nice weather we are having". Whoever was on the other side seemed to know exactly what they were doing, which of course excited Allen. The final trial was a live rabbit. The animal hopped through the blue glowing portal and 5 minutes later hopped back out completely fine. This was history in the making! Live organisms could successfully travel to other dimensions through the bridge!

The only problem was that the last sign of contact with the other side was 2 weeks ago, with nothing since.

All attempts to hail the other side for permission since then went unanswered. This worried Allen. If he couldn't get access from the other side, the next stage of human trials couldn't go on. But just as he was giving up hope, the red light on his control panel clicked on. This red light, the one he had never seen come on before could only mean 1 thing. 1 very important, life changing thing- The other side was trying to send something to them first. Every time something was sent through the bridge it had initially been sent from our dimension. This time, the other side was starting the process.

This was so exciting to Allen. He could hardly wait to push the button below the red light that would give them the okay to open the bridge; but just as he went to do so, he stopped. A distant pop pop sounded out from a distance outside of the facility. Then another, and another. If Allen didn't know any better he would have thought them to be gunshots. But gunshots here? At this secure government facility? That didn't make any sense. The only reason for shots would be someone was trying to break in, but how could they? The facility was hidden in the wilderness in the mountains of northern New York's Adirondacks. There were no population centers near and the facility was manned by 5 armed guards patrolling the area. Steel link fence topped with electrified razor wire surrounded the area along with motion sensors around the perimeter. Who would WANT to try to take the facility?

Allen shrugged it off. It was probably nothing to worry about. It must be hunters straying too close to the facility. It wouldn't be the first time it had happened. Last time, the head of security had to arrest a man who stumbled upon the facility by mistake tracking a deer. Although no population centers were near, people will always be around. That's one thing about humans, they were everywhere. He had trust in his security team; perhaps a bit too much trust.

The shots continued and grew louder, sounding now from within the building. Something was going on. Allen reached for his radio to the guard post and spoke.

"What's going on out there? Is everything okay?"

No reply. He became fearful of what he didn't know; but soon Allen's questions would be answered.

"Ghost 1 is down! I say again, Ghost 1 is down!" yelled a guard from outside the door, just down the hall as more shots rang out from his mp5 submachine gun.

"Ghost lead is gone too! Get to the lab and lock it down!" yelled another guard. The government guard then yelled in pain as shots from further down the hall sounded. The sounds of bullets pinging off the metal walls were heard by Allen and his staff, as well as the footfalls of the final surviving guard running to the lab. The man sprinted down the hallway, the door flew open and he ran in. Just as he got into the room a bullet pierced the back of his head blowing a hole through his neat black cap and bursting out the front of his skull, splattering the computer monitors with gore. Then the shooting stopped.

Moments passed and the slow sound of men walking came from down the hall. Next, 3 men strolled into the room. The lead man, middle aged and wearing a blood stained white shirt, tattered jeans, and a camouflage boonie hat came into the room. A crooked smile came across his salt and pepper bearded face as he looked down at the dead guard and spat chewing tobacco on his corpse. Then he looked up at Allen, still with his crooked smile.

"Hello Doctor. You're going to help us meet God."

TWO

"QRF has arrived" came the voice of the Lieutenant over the radio.

It had been 45 minutes since the report of the Facility 12 being attacked came to command, and since then they had learned that terrorists had taken the facility. To make matters worse, the terrorists were also holding its scientists hostage. Command had immediately ordered the quick reaction force made up of 12 army rangers to go take back the facility. They were shipped out from the closest base, Fort Hodge, which was named after the man who oversaw this fort, Colonel Hodge. The fort had also been nicknamed "Ghost Town" by the men who were stationed there. Much like Facility 12, Ghost Town was a top secret military base only 14 clicks away from Facility 12. The fact that nobody knew about it besides the government and 150 men and women stationed there made the name Ghost Town very fitting for the fort.

At the facility, the guards were all dead. All that remained were the staff of 5 scientists and the 8 heavily armed terrorists that now ran the facility. Even before the full briefing, Staff Sergeant John Rodriguez knew exactly who had taken the facility. It was a cult of Christian extremists out of the central United States known as, The Chosen. A bunch of fucking nut jobs, John thought.

It all started during the pandemic. Everyone had their own way of coping with almost an eighth of the world's population dying. Drinking, making the world a better place, finding god; but these assholes took finding god to a whole new level. Throughout the pandemic, these people would preach the word of god while trying to track down anyone they deemed "unchosen" by the lord, and murdered them brutally as sacrifice. An unchosen could be anyone gay, anyone of other beliefs, or just anyone who stood against them or wasn't white. Apparently they missed the whole memo of "thou shall not kill". The government had a hell of a time trying to stop these lunatics over the past year and half. Their version of activism was nail bombing peaceful protests or abducting minorities off the street. Hell, one of these assholes even managed to kill a senator at a rally for being a democrat. All it took was a sniper round to the neck. The psycho and his men put up a fight against SWAT for 4 hours in an apartment building before they were killed; and even though most of the world knew they were bat shit crazy, their movement was gaining more and more supporters every day. This time, they hit the government where it hurt.

"Okay listen up because i'm not going to repeat myself." the Lieutenant said. "We are going to split into two teams. My team will hold the perimeter of the facility while Sergeant Rodriguez and his team will clear out the facility and rescue the scientists."

"Fucking figures." John whispered to the man next to him, his best friend and squad mate, Specialist Joe Pots. The two men were as close as brothers. John was even the godfather of Pots' son. They had been through everything together, from Iraq to the pandemic. Pots was even there for John when he struggled with PTSD after losing his wife to the virus while on deployment. That said a lot about the man. Then on the other hand there was Bryar. It was no secret that Lieutenant Bryar was a pussy. He would always be the first one to claim the safe job while sending his men into the meat grinder. It had been this way all through their service together. In Iraq, John would always have to lead men to their deaths while he narrowly got out alive, while Bryar sat cozy in a building or a vehicle, protected by all his men. John wasn't even sure he had ever seen Bryar enter a firefight. He usually just sat back and radioed commands. Things had always been this way and it looked like this mission would be no different.

"Rodriguez, take your men through the main entrance after my men clear the outside, and then work your way to the lab. Command says to arrest if we get the opportunity because these men are still Americans, but I'm saying fuck that. The more of these psycho fucks we kill, the better." The Lieutenant was a man of many issues. Although being a complete pussy was one of them, another was his temper getting the best of him in combat. In Iraq, he had seen the man beat a prisoner half to death just for spitting on him. Luckily for him the higher ups were willing to look the other way, but here he was going at it again; but for once, John actually agreed with his orders. 8 months ago while handing out food at a FEMA camp in Kansas, he saw something he would never be able to un-see. One of these bastards had gone on a killing spree in a children's hospital tent with a spiked cross. His reason? They were Latino. The thought made John sick and he would be happy to put a bullet in one of these fucks.

The men all unloaded from their black, unmarked, government trucks and their troop transport truck. They then set up positions outside the facility gate. A sniper armed with a suppressed mk14 set up in a tree outside the fence. Sweat ran down John's tan, scarred face as the hot, July sun beat down on his black tactical armor and helmet. He and his 5 other men that made up his team took knees in a line against the front gate waiting for the order to go while QRF team 2 did the same on the opposite side of the gate. Behind Bryar, John saw where The Chosen had tunneled under the fence, avoiding the sensors and razor wire. These men were getting crafty. John didn't want to think about what else they could be capable of.

Through his binoculars he saw 2 men guard the front entrance. They seemed to be armed with AK-47s and wore ratty, torn clothing, stained with blood. The Chosen were known for desecrating bodies after killing them by skinning a cross into their chests, which is most likely how these men got so dirty. Sure enough, 5 feet to their right, John spotted a dead guard strung up from a light post, naked with blood pooling on the ground below him. The deep, crimson "t" was visible across his midsection. It made John sick and he couldn't wait to see them drop like flies.

The sound of two suppressed shots were heard and then John was given the order to move up. In tactical formation his team and the second team moved up through the gate together. The second team broke off and took positions surrounding the building and John's team moved to the front entrance. Blood was splattered against the walls with the two bodies of the terrorists slumped down in front of the doors. The sniper in the trees had made quick work of the men. John's team stepped over them and continued into the facility. This mission would prove to be a cake walk. These terrorists were very untrained and sloppy.

As they moved down the hall, two more enemies were already waiting for them and opened up with a volley of shots from their AKs before they came around the corner. These shots were a little early, which proved how sloppy and undisciplined these men were. John had guessed that the enemies had known something was up when the men out front hadn't answered their radio. This was no longer a stealth operation.

"Contacts, east hallway. Currently taking fire." Pots reported over the radio to Bryar.

"All clear out here. Permission to engage" replied Bryar.

"No fucking shit its clear there, pussy." muttered Pots under his breath. Flurries of bullets blasted the concrete wall to the right of QRF team 1. Chunks of rock flew in all directions.

"Macho, Zebra. On my go you two move up while I cover you." John said. He looked back at his two men for a response. Macho was a masculine man who stood about 6'7 and was built like a tank, hence his nickname. Zebra on the other hand was much smaller. Shortest of their ranks by far, but he got his name from how he always talked shit to everyone saying he would someday get his stripes and outrank them. This talk was annoying to most people, but John always found it entertaining and named him Zebra.

With hand signals counting down from 3 to 1, John turned the corner and opened fire with his M4 in short bursts. As he shot, the 2 enemies ducked behind cover and Zebra and Macho moved up. The enemies were pinned down by oncoming fire behind a flipped over steel table they had set up as cover, but it wasn't enough; these men had watched 1 too many movies. The force of the bullets leaving John's rifle punched through the table and blew a hole through the throat of a chubby man in overalls, his long beard settling back down, covering the gaping hole where his adam's apple should have been. Zebra and Macho shot as they moved up and peppered the remaining man with about 10 rounds, turning his body to swiss cheese. The two soldiers stopped at the bodies and gave the all clear sign to move up. Pots and John moved up after them followed by Rookie, whose name should be obvious, and Rogers, a hard ass who hated nicknames.

Rookie was a young soldier who didn't look any older than 19. This was his first mission with the team, replacing their breacher after losing him in their previous mission. The team had been deployed to Philadelphia where they were to breach a building full of The Chosen, who had taken up there for an attack. The mission was to capture a high valued target. Before their breacher, Daniels, could blast open the door, he was peppered with bullets as the targets shot through the wooden frame. Bad Intel from Colonel Hodge was given to the team and they walked into a trap. John would be damned if he would let the same fate happen to Rookie.

The 6 men moved toward the lab door and set up position to breach. John set up a snake camera and ran it under the door. As he peered around the room he saw all of the scientists, and just 1 terrorist all alone holding a pistol to one's head. He knew they were outside and he was ready for them.

"Rookie, Rogers. We are missing 3 targets. Move through the facility and take them out. The rest of you, on me" John said. Rookie and Rogers moved away down the next hall towards the conference room on the hunt while John grabbed the door handle. They stepped in, rifles up and ready to fire.

"Why hello, hello, hello there, soldier boy" said the man holding the scientist. He seemed to be the one in charge of the group of enemies. The man's deep, crackling voice paired perfectly with his appearance. The man gave a crooked smile which showed off his yellow teeth with a couple missing.

"Let the scientist go, drop the gun, and nobody has to die." John said.

"Well that's just not gonna happen, son. You see, I gots me a prophecy to fulfill."

"Prophecy? What the hell are you talking about?" John asked, agitated. He knew this was going to be some looney shit he was about to hear.

"That's right, boy. God's will. We have been chosen and we need to fulfill our destiny. These scientists here are our flock and we are the shepherds that will lead them to the light!" the man laughed. He was talking crazy, but continued. "These men, these GLORIOUS men" he said shaking the scientists who had tears pouring out of his eyes. "These men have shown us the way!"

"The way? The way to what? Just put the gun down, man!" yelled John.

"The way to the kingdom of heaven." the man stopped smiling and took a serious tone.

"He's talking about the bridge. He wants me to open the bridge!" cried the scientist.

"That's right, I mean the bridge! Bridge, *Portal*" he said sarcastically "the gate to the Kingdom of Heaven! And now, you're gonna open it for me Mr. Science man!"

"I...I can't! You don't know what you're doing!" cried the scientist.

"Oh I know exactly what I'm doing! I am following my destiny! Now do it!" the man spat as he yelled at his hostage, his finger twitching close to the trigger of the gun, dangerously close to the scientist's head. The scientist reached over and pressed the button to open the bridge. A blinding, bright blue flash happened and behind the man, the bridge appeared. Its shimmering blue waves floated in midair, shining bright light out into the entire room.

"I can drop this mother fucker now, boss. Give me the order." said Pots.

"WAIT! DON'T SHOOT!" yelled the scientist. "The bridge's arc harnesses the energy of our dimension into one point! If it's damaged while it's open it'll allow more bridges to randomly open all over the world!" he was referring to the metal ring around the bridge. This ring alone was what stopped the bridge from going haywire and causing all sorts of hell for the world.

"Oh really now? THAT I didn't know…" said the man quietly, clearly thinking to himself.

"God fucking damn it" thought John. Why did the egghead just go and admit all of that? Before anyone could say anything else, the terrorist snapped back to attention. What happened next was too fast to stop.

"THOUGH I WALK THROUGH THE VALLEY OF THE SHADOW OF DEATH, I WILL FEAR NO EVIL!" The man yelled as he dropped his hostage and shot the arc harnessing the bridge.

"No!" yelled the scientist. Before the scientist even hit the ground, Pots fired 3 rounds into the man's chest and gore exploded out his back onto the wall behind him. As he lay on the ground, the bridge opened wider and the metal ring around it burst from the bullets that tore through it, damaging its fragility. The terrorist laid slouched over himself on the floor in the corner of the room. Blood drooled from his mouth all over the front of his white shirt and down his beard. He cackled as he drew crosses all over the walls around him with his fingers, smearing the walls with his dark, clotting blood. Even in the face of death he remained completely insane. He had completed his mission.

"What have you done?" sobbed the scientist.

The nearly dead man slouched in the corner, smiled and slowly raised his head, speaking quietly.

"We are all going to see God now."

THREE

"Did that shit really just happen?" said Pots, his nervous voice trembling.

"What the fuck did that prick just do?" said Macho, also sounding nervous. John felt the same as his men, but the only one in the room who wasn't acting scared of the large blue, waving, light in the middle of the room was Zebra. He just stood there with the same arrogant smirk on his face he always had.

"Well that crazy fuck sure got what was coming to him! What the hell do you all look so upset about?" Zebra said.

"Are you fucking kidding me, Zebra? What the hell do you think we are upset about? We have a real fucking problem on our hands!" Pots yelled. Pots and Zebra had never gotten along due to Zebra's arrogance, and now was not the time to be pissing Pots off.

"What? It's not like the doc here can't just turn the damn thing off! It's technology for Christ sake!" Zebra said with an arrogant chuckle. John needed to have a talk with the man later about taking situations seriously while on the job.

"Were you not listening to the scientist a minute ago, dipshit? He can't! It's broken! That crazy fuck shot it up!" Pots yelled, clearly getting frustrated with his teammate and the situation that they had ended up in.

"For real? I thought that was just a lie to get the dude to chill out?" Zebra said, now seeing the seriousness of the situation.

"It-It's true." said the scientist. "The bridge is made up of the fabric of our dimension. It's naturally occurring energy all around us. You just can't see it. We built the arc to harness this energy and manipulate it. Once it's activated, it's held to one area. But without the arc to hold it-" the scientist trailed off.

"And just who are you exactly?" Macho asked.

"I'm Doctor Allen, the head researcher at this facility." the scientist said.

"Well that's just awesome! Even the head guy can't fix this fuck up!" Pots yelled.

"QRF 1 to QRF 2. We have a major problem." John said into his radio. He was not sure exactly how he would word this report. This situation was crazy. The argument around him continued.

"Without the arc, bridges can open all over the world. Randomly at any time. This is awful." Allen said, near sobbing. As the men pondered amongst themselves how to handle the situation they heard a dying cackle from the corner.

"Ah-you all-will see now." It was the terrorist still alive in the corner, bleeding out, taking labored breaths between words. "God-is-coming. You all-will-see."

"Listen you bastard-" Macho started to yell but stopped. Something was happening with the bridge. The sound of rushing air filled the room and the bright blue light that shimmered off of the rippling portal darkened.

"Something is coming through." said Allen, eyes wide in preparation for what was coming. The men all stood there waiting. With a sudden gust of air and a flash, a man came running through the bridge. He wore fatigues and a Kevlar vest, loaded with magazines of ammunition. A green ball cap on his head said "Marines". He had a short, brown beard that looked ungroomed, like he hadn't gotten to shave for weeks. In his arms he carried a decked out M4 carbine and he aimed it around the room. Too shocked to do anything after seeing one of their own men come out of the bridge, the QRF team just sat there in awe. The marine only had one thing to say as he came out of the portal.

"You all need to run!" he said as he bolted out of the lab.

"You never said anything about having sent troops through the bridge" John said, completely caught off guard by what just happened. Nobody in the room seemed to be phased at all by what the marine had said.

"I-I-" Allen stuttered. "I didn't send people through-" he stopped as another flash happened and this time a group came running out. A dozen civilians and half a dozen soldiers came running out of the bridge panting heavily. The last two soldiers to come through were spattered with blood. These people all looked terrified and also yelled to run as they sprinted out of the lab.

"What the fuck." was all that John managed to say before another blood stained soldier appeared out of the bridge.

"They are coming! Close the bridge! Close the goddamn bridge!" the man said, waving his arms frantically in front of the bridge.

"Who-" John started to ask before the man screamed in agony. John had never heard a man scream like that in all of his life. He had seen mortal wounds on the battlefield, people tortured and in pain, but this was a scream of raw fear.

The man who had just come through the bridge, now had a pair of clawed, pale arms grab his ankles and pull. He flopped to the floor, drew his M9 holstered at his hip and turned to fire while screaming; but he was too slow. The arms dragged him across the floor back into the bridge as he screamed at the top of his lungs.

"God, don't let them get me!" he cried as he disappeared into the bridge, leaving a blood smeared trail from where he was dragged. This snapped the QRF back to reality and they all raised their rifles to the rippling blue void.

"Rookie, Rogers. Get your asses back to the lab now!" John yelled into the radio. He continued to speak to the other men, now. "Get ready men. I don't know what the fuck is going on but I don't like it."

The soldiers all prepared for what was to come out of the bridge next. The bridge flashed a final time and this time, instead of people running out, came these….

Creatures. Pale, grey flesh covered their muscular bodies. They resembled humans but were more animalistic. At the tip of their long, thick fingers were sharp black claws, many of which were coated with a layer of what appeared to be blood. As disturbing as the sight was, nothing was even close to how terrifying their faces were. Scrawny faces with bloodshot eyes looked eagerly around the lab room. The creatures' mouths were lined with white, needle-like teeth. Facial features remained unique as well as their hair, which made them seem somewhat human, but it was quite obvious these creatures were far from it.

Through the bridge came 5, then 10, and next thing they knew there were 20 of the animalistic beings entering the lab from the bridge. They stood and looked around the room at first, seeming confused. Then, as if they had all sensed the new presence at the same time, the creatures all focused on the group of people in the room in sync. One of the doctors closest to the portal gasped and stumbled backwards, tripping and falling onto the floor. The sudden movement attracted the attention of 3 of the creatures and they pounced onto the man.

"Oh god help me!" the scientist screamed as one of the creatures bit down on his right calf muscle. The needle teeth of the creature pierced through his flesh like a hot knife in butter. The creature dragged its clamped jaw down the man's leg tearing away a hunk of skin, muscle and ligament. The man screeched in horror as the other two creatures did the same to his arms, leaving him helpless and unable to fight back.

"Holy shit! Take them down!" yelled John, still not believing what he was seeing. His men opened fire, cutting down the first line of the monsters. 5.56 NATO rounds tore through the flesh of the monsters, spattering the wall behind them with brains and blood. It looked like a mosaic art show. John picked his targets and fired his rifle on semi-automatic, trying to keep his aim precise. They had cut down at least 10 of the monsters but they just kept coming out of the bridge, and now they were on a dead sprint towards the men.

"The prophecy has come to pass. It's the coming of a new age!" the terrorist managed to yell out as his last words before he was torn apart by the creatures. Over the gunshots and growling John heard his crazed laughter turn to screams of agony.

"Keep firing! Keep firing! Protect the scientists!" John yelled, a little too late. As he spoke the horde of teeth and claws piled on top of another scientist who let out an ear piercing, high pitched cry. She disappeared under the mound and nothing was seen except her hand hanging out, twitching and the red ropes flying all across the room, which John thought were her intestines.

"Holy shit! We can't hold them!" yelled Zebra, who had finally seemed to run out of jokes as he watched the horror unfold in front of him.

"Fall back! Get the fuck out of here!" John yelled as he fired the last 4 rounds of his magazine into a beast diving across the room at him. It was fast, but not fast enough as the bullets tore through its gaping mouth and burst out the back of its skull sending chunks of bone into the horde.

The men fell back into the outside hall covering the movement of the scientist who remained. Outside of the lab was the group of people from the portal, just trying to figure out where to go.

"Move!" yelled Pots as they ran out of the lab. The team had no idea who these people were, but they weren't going to stand by as they all were slaughtered. John ran to the front of the group and ordered them to follow him. The group started to run towards the exit of the building when they heard banging overhead.

"They got into the fucking vents!" Macho yelled as he angled his M4 up towards the ceiling. Behind him Zebra had been the last one out of the lab.

"We gotta get out of here, man! Every man for himself!" he yelled as he turned to run. Wrong move. He tripped over his own feet in his panic. Before he was even 5 feet out of the lab doorway the horde chasing him tackled him to the ground. He didn't even have time to scream. One of the beasts bit his throat and tore out his windpipe. It hung out of its mouth like a sausage. The group kept running.

As they approached the exit, the overhead vent gave out ahead of them and a handful of the creatures toppled to the floor, cutting their escape off. Before they had time to react, a vent above the group collapsed as well, dropping a pair of beasts onto one of the soldiers from the bridge. They were clawing at him before they even landed. The animalistic behavior of these creatures was startling.

The group scattered in all directions looking for a place to run to. John, as well as the majority of the group, ran down the hall to the conference room. As he ran he looked back at the group that split away. Pots and several of the people from the bridge ran the other direction towards the security room. Macho still stood in place shuffling his feet, trying to decide where to go; a decision that took far too long. Two groups of the beasts grabbed him from two sides. He screamed in agony as they pulled the two halves of his body in opposite directions, ripping the poor man in half. John had to look away.

"Holy shit, holy shit, and holy shit." he said to himself as he ran. As his group rounded the corner, they bumped into Rookie and Rogers.

"We saw the terrorists headed towards the medical bay-" Rookie said as John cut him off.

"Screw that. Missions over! Run!" John said running by.

"Wha-" Rookie said as he saw what they were running from. "What the fuck are those things!" he exclaimed, raising his M1014 shotgun to firing position and let off 3 rounds of buckshot into the approaching creatures, smashing their skulls apart like pumpkins.

"Don't shoot, just move!" John yelled as he and the group disappeared around the corner of the hall. Rookie stopped firing and ran behind them, but Rogers kept on firing. He stood his ground and blasted into the hoard with his M4 set to full auto. Within seconds his gun clicked as the magazine was empty. As he took the time to change magazines he was run over by the beasts and not even his scream was heard over the growls of the oncoming beasts.

John, still on a dead sprint as they were being pursued, led the group into the large conference room. Everyone ran in, with Rookie being the final one to enter. John slammed the doors shut. He and the marine from the bridge both quickly barricaded the doors with a table, several chairs and backed away from the doors with their rifles aimed at the mound of blockage. Outside of the door they heard the creatures in the hall growling out of hunger. They slammed the doors over and over again trying to get in but weren't budging the barricade.

John looked around the room at all of the people. In the room with him he had Rookie, who now sat against the wall panting, 2 of the soldiers from the bridge, Doctor Allen, and 9 of the civilians from the bridge. There were many people missing from this group including Pots. Last he saw, his friend was leading 2 soldiers and 2 civilians in the opposite direction when the group broke up. He could only pray that they were okay. As for the rest of the missing people, he had no idea where they were.

For a moment, the creatures outside had quit slamming the door and gave the room silence. This frightened John. He could hear the beasts standing outside the door still in the hall. The only thing separating the group from the hungry horde was a set of wooden doors and a brick wall. Could these things think? Were they planning something? John wasn't sure, but he knew he needed to process everything that just happened over the past few minutes. Once John had cleared his head he turned to the marine from the bridge and said- "What is going on and who the hell are you?"

<u>FOUR</u>

The marine stared in disbelief at the question, as if it was the most uncalled for question he had ever heard.

"I hardly think we have time for stories and introductions right now, Staff Sergeant. There are much bigger problems going on." the marine finally answered.

John couldn't believe the answer he was given. Either this man was extremely difficult or very stupid. Why the mysterious man was leading a group of battered civilians and soldiers out of an interdimensional portal trailed by man-eating beasts was definitely not an uncalled for question.

"Listen, shithead. I just watched 3 of my teammates get brutally torn apart by god knows what, so forgive my request for story time, but how about you show me a little god damn respect and tell me who the fuck you are!" John snapped back at the man.

The man stood silent, glaring into John's eyes. He had the look of someone who had watched the whole world burn. John saw the hate and anger in the eyes of the man who looked like he hadn't slept for days. For a second John forgot about the situation going on around him and he felt pity for the man he had just verbally attacked. Before he could ponder the situation further the man spoke.

"My name is 2nd Lieutenant Steve Miller, United States Marine Corps." the man finally said. "I am aware how you must be feeling right now, and believe me, I get it.”

"You just came out of the bridge. With all of these people; and all of those- things.” John said.

"Yes we did. We are not of your dimension. It's a very long story we don't have time for, but to sum it up, our situation is fucked up. Majorly fucked up.” Said Miller with a look of horror coming to his face as he mentally re-lived everything that he had seen prior to the bridge.

"Okay, you're not from here. What is going on? Where are you from? Who are all of these people? You still haven't told me what the fuck is going on! What are those things!” John exclaimed, still frustrated.

"Our dimension is gone. Overran. Everyone and everything there is dead. We are all that remain. We are refugees. We are-” Miller began to explain before John cut him off, clearly shocked.

"Gone? Gone, what do you mean it's gone? Surely you don't mean this is the last of humanity. The OTHER humanity. No more than 20 people came out of the bridge!” John said, his voice shaking from fear.

Miller took a long deep breath, held it in, and slowly let it out. He was clearly trying not to lose his mind. "Yes. This is all that is left. Everyone else is gone. The bridge was a last ditch effort at survival for these people.” he said slowly and patiently.

"Jesus Christ.” John replied. He couldn't conjure further words for what Miller had said. They sat in silence for an agonizing 10 seconds before John spoke again. "And those things, what are they?"

"Those things aren't things per say. They are people- were people." Miller said quietly looking at the floor, eyes wide.

"I thought you said everyone was gone? Dead?" John asked in confusion.

"They are dead. They are gone. They are not human any longer. Do those things still look like people to you?" Miller replied. John thought back on the first one he saw come out of the bridge. It clearly resembled a human but was very different. The teeth, the claws, the skin, eyes. They even looked larger and more predator-like.

"No. No they don't. So what are you saying they are? Zombies? Is this some Hollywood horror shit?" John said.

"Zombies? No. No no no. These things aren't zombies. Zombies would be too easy. These things? These are much, much worse."

Before Miller could share any more about the situation, the banging outside the door started again. The men snapped back to the reality of the situation.

"Brace those doors! Don't let them get inside or we are dead!" Miller shouted to his people. The people from the other dimension. The others.

"QRF 1 to QRF 2. We need backup ASAP! The situation has drastically changed!" John shouted into his radio. Seconds later the reply came through.

"QRF 2 to QRF 1. We have to hold position on the perimeter. Your professionals. You can handle whatever it is." Bryar replied.

"QRF 1 to QRF 2. We need backup now! The situation-" John yelled in anger before he was cut off.

"Listen, Staff Sergeant, if we don't hold the perimeter more of those cultists could get in. You can handle the situation. Bryar out."

John was livid. Clearly Bryar had no clue what was going on in here and was sitting silently outside. He wouldn't even give John the chance to explain what was going on and cut him off!

"Listen you fucking pussy-" John started to say over coms to Bryar when a loud bang stopped him. But it wasn't the door. The monsters outside continued to slam into the door and its barricade but the loud bang came from the other end of the room. Then he heard it again and again. Then suddenly the vent cover from the floor burst off and the slim, bent piece of metal flew across the room hitting the wall, clanking onto the floor. John and another soldier turned from the chaos at the door and looked at the vent just in time to see a pair of clawed, bloodied arms reach out from the vent and grab a woman's ankles. She screamed as its claws dug into her flesh. She fought all she could to not be dragged into the dark hole in the floor, kicking and trying to plant her feet; but that ended when the creature's clawed thumb slit her Achilles tendon. She yelped a high pitch squeal as she felt her tendons snap like rubber bands and shoot up into her legs. From her ankle a fleshy piece of tendon waved around splattering her blood all over the chairs next to her. Her legs gave out, unable to support her fighting and she collapsed to the floor. Now being dragged back towards the vent she clawed at the hard wood floor trying to find something, anything, to grab onto. She clawed so hard at the floor that her fingers trailed blood from where she had skinned her fingertips trying to fight the beast.

"Somebody help me!" she cried. Then, in one final tug before anyone could do anything, the beast dragged her down into the hole where her screams of agony and horror faded out.

"It's a trap! The ones at the door are distracting us!" yelled Miller. Just as he said that another beast crawled completely from the vent and charged into the crowd. Miller raised his rifle and put a round into the creature's right eye socket. It dropped to the floor a few feet ahead of Allen, who was curled into a ball rocking back and forth, crying. Then out of the vent came another, and then another. Miller and John focused fire onto the vent while the rest of the group held the door. Those next moments would lead to the doom of every person stuck inside that room.

FIVE

Pots ran as fast as he could down the hall with the people he led. With a quick glance behind him he saw 4 people following his fast paced sprint. He also noticed that the rest of the group had split off in different directions after the creatures ambushed them all from the vents, ruining their fast, easy escape. The upside was that while most of the creatures had continued chasing the main group, only a few had broken away to chase Pots. He looked forward and continued running around the corner of the hallway. Straight ahead he saw the open door that led to the security room for the facility. The open door may as well have been a golden gate to Pots, who was desperate for any sort of cover to hide in.

"Quick, get into the security room!" Pots yelled at the group as he stopped and turned around at the door to cover them.

Around the corner the 3 creatures chasing them slid into one another, eager to sink their teeth into their next new meal. Pots raised his M4 and fired off 4 rounds. The first two hit their targets center mass. One shot kills, clean as ever. The bullets smacked into their chests and dropped the beasts like flies. The 3rd shot clipped a beast in its shoulder, but it kept barreling forward like it didn't even feel the pain of the round. Pots' 4th and final shot went right between the beast's eyes, punching a golf ball sized hole out the back of its head leaving pink chunks of brain matter all around its body in the hall. Those appeared to be the only beasts giving chase to the group, but Pots didn't want to stick around to find out. He quickly lowered his gun, stepped into the room, and shut the door.

The security room was a small, grey area that had just enough room to comfortably fit the 5 people. Pots looked around at the area and welcomed the safety of the new hiding spot. Ahead of him were several monitors that displayed all of the halls of the facility, and the building exterior. Pots leaned against the wall, took his helmet off, and caught his breath. He needed a few seconds to take in what had happened in the hall. It all happened so fast. One moment the lab was quiet, the next they were running for their lives. What had happened in between? Was everyone alright?

"No, not everyone was alright" he thought, remembering Zebra's brutal death. It was true that Pots never liked the kid, but he didn't wish him to die; but it wasn't just Zebra. He thought he saw Macho die as well when he ran away. Ripped in half. A horrible way to go. Who else had died? Did John die as well?

"No, no way." He thought. He hadn't seen John go down. Last he knew he was leading the group. Anyway, John was too good a fighter to go down easy. Nobody knew his friend better than he did. He knew that John was a dedicated soldier and leader. Pots and John had been together for 8 years. 8 full years of active duty in the United States Army. The shit that they had seen over the years together created a bond like no other between the men. John had saved Pots' life on multiple occasions. One specific incident came to mind. The team had been pinned down by insurgents in Iraq. There seemed to be no way out of the mess they had gotten themselves into. The mission was simple; take a suspected Al Qaeda hideout located just inside Fallujah. The team had been so close when their point man was hit with a sniper round. Gunfire had erupted from all over around them and that was when they realized they had walked into an ambush. Pots had been hit in his right chest with a round and dropped. All of the men thought they were dead. Backup was too far out. But then John had stepped up. He laid down covering fire while he barked orders to his men to do the same. One by one the men managed, somehow, to escape back to allied ground with their lives through a back alleyway. John was the last one to leave, carrying Pots on his shoulders the entire way. That was their first mission together ever. He would never forget it. Pots even made John his son's godfather 4 years after that day. His son was also close with John; that was, until his son had passed away after contracting the virus a year ago. That had hurt Pots and put him in a dark place, but John was there for him. Even after John lost his wife to the same virus, he remained by Pots' side. The two were the best of friends.

The moment of thoughts of past events faded away quickly as one of the soldiers in the security room spoke and snapped Pots back to reality.

"That was a close one. My names Edwards. Private First Class Jake Edwards, sir." the young man said, holding out his hand to greet Pots.

"No offense Edwards, but now is not the time." Pots said, ignoring the offer for a handshake. He didn't intend to be mean to the kid, but now really wasn't the time.

Pots looked around the room again and examined his motley crew. He had two soldiers with him. One, Edwards, who looked about 18 and held an expression of youthful hope mixed with terror. The other had to have been in his mid-30's and sat expressionless. His mouth sat straight and unmoved within his black, shaggy beard. This guy had seen some serious shit. To the right of the men was a young child, maybe 7. She sat in a chair with her eyes full of tears as, who had to have been her father, sat by her side trying to comfort her. Pots felt sorry for what the girl had seen but needed to focus.

"I see there are cameras here showing the facility. Let's take a look and see how fucked we are." Pots said as he approached the monitors.

On the first screen he saw QRF team 1. They paced around the facility, patrolling the area for any further targets. Bryar was casually leaning against a wall. What happened in here clearly had not happened there yet.

"Lucky for Bryar." he thought as he rolled his eyes. He doubted they even knew what was going on, but doubted he would make an attempt to help if he did. Regardless, Pots had lost his radio during the retreat, so backup was out of the question.

On several other monitors Pots had noticed there were still people roaming the halls. Some cautiously, others, not so much. It seemed there were stragglers from the groups who had been lost. Pots intensely watched the screens as the people tried to escape.

Two scientists were running through the halls frantically trying to find an exit that didn't lead to death. The two women still wore their white, and now red, blood soaked lab coats. According to the audio from the video feed, there didn't seem to be any creatures near them. The women were quietly arguing amongst themselves what to do.

"Those things are everywhere! What have we done! Oh god!" the one woman sobbed.

"Shut up!" the other woman hissed quietly. "They will hear us and I don't want to die."

The women kept running, their heavy footfalls echoing down the hallway. As if that wasn't loud enough, the sobbing woman rushed to a closet and whipped the door open. As soon as she did, buckets and mops came tumbling out of the small space and banged all over the floor.

"What the fuck are you doing!" the other woman hissed again.

"We need to hide! I can't take it! I need to hide!" the sobbing woman yelled in panic.

Just then, before the other woman could argue, a crazed yelling sounded from down the hall, animalistic sounding and hungry.

"Oh fuck!" yelled the sobbing woman as she slammed the door shut on her coworker. The coworker took off running only to be tackled by a beast and cried shrieks of agony as the beast bit her face and peeled it away, swallowing the flesh and leaving a bloody mess of bone still alive and screaming. They then slammed themselves against the closet door rapidly as the sobbing woman inside yelled.

"Go away! I'm not supposed to die here!" she cried. Too little too late. One beast crashed through the door and, not visible to the camera, was torn to shreds. All that was seen was pooling blood running out into the hall from the closet.

Pots shuddered at the sight. Those poor women couldn't make it out alive. He glanced to his right and saw the man and his child staring at the screen in horror.

"Sir" Pots said to the man as calmly as he could. "Please don't let your daughter see this." She had already seen so much but he wouldn't let her see more if it could be helped.

Pots looked over to another screen where he saw 3 men dressed in ratty flannel shirts, mesh hats, and dirtied jeans running for the main lobby of the facility.

"Those fucking cultists" he said to himself.

The 3 men ran as fast as they could to the main doors of the lobby.

"What in the hell was that fuckin' thang?" the man in the back said in confusion. "It got you pretty good." He continued, gesturing at the man next to him. The man was holding his gut, which was dripping blood all over the floor as he ran.

"Fuckin' thang slash my gut! With its big ass claws!" the man yelled, clearly in extreme pain.

"Fuck what the boss says. This shit aint holy. I'm out!" the 3rd man said.

The 3 men kept running and the wounded man began to slow down from blood loss, finally getting a hold of him.

"Hurry the fuck up, Earl! We need to leave now!" the lead man exclaimed. They were almost to the doors and so close to freedom.

"I-I-I can't-" the wounded man said, his voice starting to trail off. He was looking pale.

"Screw you! I am leavin'!" yelled the lead man. As he turned, a creature burst out from a side room next to him and tackled him to the wall. Its teeth clamped around his neck as he yelled.

"Holy hell!" yelled the other man who quickly raised his shotgun and pumped a slug into the creature's back. The large round tore through the beast and left a gaping hole from its back to its chest you could see through, but in his panic he hadn't realized that the shot also had burst through his buddy. The two bodies laid slumped against the wall on top of each other, their innards laying around them like ground hamburger.

"I'm sorry, Earl, I gotta go!" the other man said, leaving his wounded teammate on the ground to bleed out. As he turned, he saw that a beast had been behind him. This one towered over him. Being at least 6'8 and built like a tank, the grey skinned beast wrapped one massive hand around the man's neck and lifted him into the air. The man kicked and swatted at the beast but it was futile. The beast quickly squeezed hard and crushed the man's neck with an audible popping sound. Then it dragged the body away to another room to feed.

The wounded man laid on the floor in a pool of his own blood. Not dead yet, but too wounded to move, he laid helplessly as another beast crouched above him. It reached into his wounded gut and grabbed his intestines. It tugged it from the man's gut as he gulped for air, too tired to scream. He watched as the beast bit down on the organ, and clambered away with it to feed, unraveling the rest of the organ and pulling it from the man's still alive body like a rope before it finally snapped.

Pots had to look away. Part of him wanted to smirk at the terrorists getting what they deserved, but the rest of him was disgusted at the sight of what had just happened. Behind him he could hear Edwards puking in the corner.

"You okay kid?" Pots asked.

"I'm fine. That's just a new one for me, that's all. Jesus Christ." the kid said, shaking his head.

Pots wanted to stop watching the cameras but he just couldn't. He knew there were more people out there still and wanted to help if he could. He also needed to know where John was. He looked over to another monitor that showed feed fairly close to the security room.

One soldier was leading around a civilian. They both had been split up from the group during the chase and were now coming out of a bathroom they had locked themselves in.

"I think they passed. I think we are in the clear." the soldier said. He slowly walked down the hall quietly, aiming his M249 SAW around as he walked. He was being as careful as he could. The bulky machine gun in his arms wasn't the best for maneuvering the halls but it would put up a hell of a fight against another swarm of the creatures. When the coast was clear he motioned for the woman he was protecting to come out of hiding. They moved down the hall slowly and quietly.

"We need to go. We need to hide." the woman said over and over. "I don't want to be here. I want to go home. I shouldn't be here." she said, hyperventilating.

"Listen to me, Rebecca. We can't hide forever. They will find us. We need to move. We have seen this before. Just stay quiet and move." the soldier said quietly. Almost so quiet that the camera couldn't catch the audio.

They moved down the hall to the corner that met the main lobby.

Pots felt himself tense up, knowing what was out there. Before they walked out further the soldier stopped.

"Let me check if it's clear." he said. Pots relaxed a tad.

The man peeked around the corner and saw the horror show that had just happened minutes before in the lobby. 5 of the creatures were sitting in there, hunched over 3 bodies and feasting on the flesh. One of the body's arms was already gnawed down to the bone by a beast. They fed fast and vigorously.

"It's not safe. We can't go this way." the soldier said as he slowly backed away from the corner. "I think I saw some people head toward the conference room. We should go there. Safety in numbers."

The pair slowly crept back the way they came and down another hall towards the conference room.

Pots looked over to another screen that showed the hall outside the conference room. It was swarmed with at least a dozen of the creatures, all pounding against the sturdy, wooden doors locked into place. There had to have been someone there.

The soldier and the woman slowly walked towards the hall of the conference room.

"Shit, they are going to get themselves killed if they go there. Edwards, how fast are you?" Pots turned and asked the Private.

"Shit, fastest in this room I would guess." Edwards replied.

"Go fast, and go now. Bring those people back here. And don't get yourself killed!" Pots ordered. Edwards nodded his head and took off running on the tip of his toes. Fast but silent. Pots really hoped he hadn't sent the kid to his death.

On the monitor Pots looked up and saw Edwards moving down the facility, avoiding all the areas with hostiles, and ran quickly to the pair. On the screen showing the other two, Pots swore under his breath as the woman tripped and tumbled to the floor. She stayed quiet but the noise seemed to draw the attention of one of the beasts. It broke off from its pack outside the conference room door and moved down the hall towards the sound.

The soldier turned his back and bent down to help the woman up.

"Are you okay?" he asked her.

"I'm fine. I am okay." she replied. The soldier let a small smile show to comfort the woman, but as he did she yelped and looked behind him.

The creature that had split off from the pack was now rushing to the pair to claim the kills and earn its meal;

but just as the creature was about to make its kill, something miraculous happened.

Edwards came rushing out around the corner of the hall from behind the woman. He saw the beast charging his fellow soldier and dropped his FN SCAR to hang by his waist at its strap. He quickly unsheathed his combat knife and bolted past the two people at the beast. Neither beast, nor human, saw him coming. He tackled the massive creature to the ground. It went flying off its feet and slammed into the tile floor. Edwards then twirled the knife in his hands and before the beast could let out a yelp, he had plunged it directly into the monster's windpipe and twisted it with a satisfying crunch. The dark blood of the beast ran out onto the floor and coated Edwards' gloves but it kept flailing, unable to yelp. He then pulled the knife and plunged it again twice as hard into the monster's left eye, dealing the final blow. Once it stopped twitching he pulled his blade, wiped it off on the beast's brown hair, and sheathed it.

"You can't go this way. I have a group, follow me." he said to the people as they turned and ran after Edwards back to safety.

"Holy shit, kids got balls." Pots found himself saying in amazement, eyes wide. He was amazed by the entire situation that just occurred but was glad he had chosen the knife. Had he shot, it for sure would have attracted more beasts and God knew how many lurked around this facility now with the bridge wide open.

A few minutes later Edwards returned with the pair in tow behind him.

"Here they are, sir. Safe as you requested." the kid said proudly and politely.

Pots smiled and shut the door behind them.

"Thank you so much. I don't know what we would have done without your help." The woman said, hugging Edwards. The kid smirked but stayed silent.

"You were headed to the conference room." Pots said. "Are there people there?"

"When the group split up I saw everyone head that way. They have to be there." said the soldier, who was catching his breath from running.

"Then that's where we want to go, together. We need to make a plan and get ready to move to save those people." Pots said, looking back at the camera feed showing a little more than a dozen creatures now slamming on the door. On audio he could swear he was hearing shooting inside. He hoped he wasn't too late to save his friend. "Get your stuff and let's go." Pots said, opening the door to move.

The crowd slowly made their way out of the security room, the soldier with the SAW taking point. As Edwards passed by, Pots stopped him and grabbed his hand for a shake.

"Pots. The names Pots." he said smiling.

<u>SIX</u>

"Fuck! We can't hold them much longer!" yelled Rookie, who was leaning intensely against the door, bracing it as hard as he could. The young, baby faced man pushed as hard as he could against the shoves from the other side. Each time a beast slammed into the door, Rookie had to stop his feet from sliding out from under him. Not only was Rick "Rookie" Smith young, but he was fairly small as well. His skinny frame was covered with toned muscle, but compared to the rest of the team, he was by far the smallest.

The beasts continued to slam against the door harder and harder each time they hit. It would only be a matter of minutes before they breached. As if that wasn't enough, John and Miller were holding off the beasts climbing through the vents at the other end of the room.

"Keep holding, Rookie! We have to hold out till help arrives!" yelled John as he fired off one shot into the temple of a beast as it poked its head out of the vent. As much as he wanted to believe help would come, he knew better. Bryar was still outside and had shut down coms between teams; and at this point he could only assume Pots and the others were dead.

The thought made him shiver. Pots was the only family he had left. If he was gone, John would be alone. He cared about his men. He wished no harm to any of them; but in his 30 years on this earth and his 8 years in the service, he had learned to get close to nobody. Every time he did, someone would die. He had seen teammate after teammate die in combat. Even on the home front he had seen his wife die, and his god son. Both he and Pots were a mess after his god son's death, but where Pots had moved on while keeping his memory alive, John had still blamed himself for not protecting him enough. To this day John still had avoided acknowledging the fact the child was gone, and avoided the topic at all costs. After all of the death he had witnessed in past years, he only stayed close to one man. The man who was a brother to him- Pots.

John shoved the thought aside for the time being and focused on the situation at hand as another beast shoved its way past the bodies in the vent and popped out at the survivors. A shot from Miller dropped it over the vent hole, but he could see multiple hands sticking up to push the body aside. They were surrounded with no way out. Suddenly they heard a loud crack.

"Shit! Sarge, the door!" Rookie shouted as he backed away from the barricade and raised his shotgun. John turned from the vent and glanced over at what Rookie was talking about. With the last shove to the door, a large crack split halfway down the door and with another slam, a beast's head busted through a new hole in the door. It snarled at Rookie and stared him down, its eyes wide and bloodshot. Its pupils spread out wide, dilated, as it looked into the face of its chosen prey. Rookie ended the creature's hopes with a 12 gauge buckshot round. The lead balls smack into the crown of the creature's head and blew its skull open, leaving its head hanging. Its skull looked like a bowl of tomato soup being dumped.

"They are in! Door is busted!" Rookie shouted. Each slam now resulted in a chunk of the door being torn away.

"Get against the back wall!" Miller yelled to the crowd. The civilians were screaming louder with each slam into the barricade and a few were hunched against the wall crying. The tears in their eyes reminded the soldiers who they were fighting for and they all stepped forward.

"They are about to get through! Focus your fire on the door and mind your ammunition! Don't let them take the civilians!" one of the soldiers shouted. She appeared to be Millers' second in command. Together, forming a perimeter in front of the civilians, John, Miller, Rookie, the two soldiers, and one of the civilians wielding a glock all raised their weapons and opened fire.

The door burst open and a horde of beasts sprinted into the room, tumbling over each other, dying to be the first one to the buffet. The soldiers all continued shooting.

"Changing mag!" the female Sergeant to John's left yelled as she dropped the magazine from her M-16 and slammed another in. She lifted her gun and fired a 3-round burst into the oncoming horde, taking down 1 beast and clipping the kneecap of another. The beast tumbled to the ground but kept crawling towards the people, as if it felt no pain.

"Stay the fuck down!" the Sergeant yelled as she stepped forward to finish the job.

"Stay in line!" Miller yelled, but the Sergeant either didn't hear him or was already committed to the task. She took several steps forward and aimed down at the wounded creature. It looked up at her and screamed a high pitch, terrifying noise. It reminded John of the sound a fisher cat made, back when he was trapping with his dad as a boy. The sound scared the shit out of him then and it made him damn near piss his pants now.

The Sergeant put a burst into the head of the wounded beast which finished the job. Bullets flew past her protecting her from the oncoming hoard behind her, but what she didn't expect was the ones coming from the vent to her left. As she began to step back to her position she was tackled into the conference room table. She smacked her head against the hardwood, and John heard the crunch from her neck snapping. She was dead; a considerably better way to go than being torn apart.

"Fuck! Keep firing!" Miller yelled to those who remained. The firing line dropped beast after beast, making the floor slick with dark blood, but more kept running down the hall and into the room.

"I'm out of ammo!" John yelled, dropping his rifle and drawing his M9, holstered at his hip. Before he could get his gun up and firing, one of the creatures knocked him off his feet and was on top of him. Its red eyes were wide as it snapped its wide, needle lined mouth inches above John's face. It tried to claw at his gut but John was holding it's hands down, using all of the strength he had. The creature growled and thrust its face hard toward John's with its mouth gaping. Just when John thought he had lost the struggle he heard a pop, and the head of the abomination jerked back and the body went limp on top of him. He shoved it aside and quickly scooted back towards the wall on his butt. He wiped the blood off of his face and looked up to see one of the civilians standing there with her glock. She had saved his life.

"Th-thank you." John said with a shaky voice.

"Don't thank me yet. We are still in this!" she yelled as she turned and popped off 3 more shots towards the door.

John stood up and raised his M9 and fired. They had stood their ground for about 45 seconds now and there still seemed to be no end to the beasts. Bodies were piling up on the floor. 10? 15? John had no idea. It was hard to tell with the swarm continuing.

"I'm out!" yelled one of the soldiers, drawing his pistol as well.

"Me too!" yelled the civilian, who now pulled a pocket knife from her blood-stained shorts. Rookie took notice of this and shifted position and stood in front of her, firing his shotgun.

"Stay behind me, ma'am." he said calmly, trying not to cause more panic than there already was. The woman looked offended by him as if she could handle the situation but there was no time to argue. They were down to 4 fighters now and were limited on ammo.

"Cover me! Changing!" Miller yelled as his gun clicked, empty. He reached down to his vest and his hands came up empty. "Shit, I'm out!" He yelled while drawing his Colt 1911.

The horde was closing in. They were swarming through the door now. John thought about everyone he had lost. His men, his wife, his god son.

"See you soon." he whispered to himself; but just before he could greet death he heard the loud cracking of automatic gunfire from down the hall. It sounded like a machine gun.

"Clear the hall and get to the conference room, fast!" yelled a man down the hall. John recognized this voice. Only one man he knew had this deep and commanding voice- Pots.

Hope rose in John.

"Maybe not this soon." he whispered again. He didn't want to die yet. Not now that he knew his friend was still alive. He and the other soldiers stepped forward and pushed towards the horde, firing. The creatures shuffled their feet in confusion not knowing where to go. Being flanked had blindsided them.

Outside the door the shooting was much closer and approaching quickly. John fired 2 more shots off into the chest of a beast as it slumped over the table, spilling its blood across the top of it, and he looked to the door which was now torn apart. Passing in front of the door he saw a soldier with a SAW firing steadily at beasts down the hall and behind him moved 2 more soldiers firing their rifles. Then into the doorway stepped Pots, followed by 3 civilians. The large man looked like an angelic being, coming just in the nick of time to lead them to safety.

"Holy shit, Pots. You're alive! You're fucking alive!" yelled John, smiling.

"Yea, but I won't be and you won't be if we don't move!" Pots replied. "We are holding them back but more are coming. Let's go!"

John and the group all ran out into the hall, stepping over the corpses and casualties of the battle that had just taken place. The conference room and hallway were littered with gore and bodies. Pots led the reunited group down the hall and towards the exit. John looked behind him at the men holding the beasts back, as the rest of the civilians and soldiers ran by. The man with the SAW was laying down with his bipod deployed, firing steadily into a horde at the end of the hall. Bullet casings flew everywhere and pinged off the concrete walls.

"Edwards, Alvarez, Move!" yelled the man with the SAW to his fellow soldiers standing by him, firing.

"What about you?" said the younger of the two men.

"Forget me Edwards! Just get those people out!" yelled the machine gunner as he fired.

"Fuck that, I'm with you, brother." said the older, bearded man as he stepped forward and fired his M4 alongside the machine gunner. "Get out of here Edwards! You're young and have a life to live once this is over!"

The young man who must have been Edwards hesitated and then ran off down the hall after the group.

John turned and ran after him. Behind him he heard shots, yelling, more shots, and then the firing stopped.

"I'm out!" yelled the machine gunner. John glanced over his shoulder before he rounded the corner and saw the horde take the two men who had given their lives so the others could escape. John heard one man scream and then heard Alvarez.

"Eat shit you nasty fucks!" Alvarez yelled, followed by an explosion. He had pulled the pin on a grenade as the horde overtook him. John turned away from the slaughter and ran.

Ahead of him he heard the shouts to get the people to move as they approached the exit. Occasionally, a shot would ring out and John would pass a dead beast that had blocked their path, but most of the creatures were behind them and catching fast. Finally the exit was in view. John heard his radio click on as he passed several corpses that had been gnawed on down to the bone.

"Shit! Rodriguez, where the fuck are you!" Bryar was yelling.

"What the fuck are those things!?" a man was yelling in the background of the message.

"Rodriguez! We need back up ASAP!" Bryar yelled with the sounds of shots over the coms. Clearly the beasts had made it outside and attacked team 2. It appeared Bryar had just found out the importance of team communication and backup.

With no time to answer the call for aid, John burst through the exit and passed the bodies of the two cultists that had guarded the entrance on the way in. Once outside, John had to stop to analyze the scene that played out before him.

Not only were creatures coming out of the vents from inside the building but from the woods a horde of the creatures were pouring out of a shimmering blue portal behind the trees. A bridge.

"Oh my god. It's already happening!" yelled Allen in horror. "It's a bridge event! It's happening!" The bridges were now opening outside of the lab, just as Allen said they would.

At the edge of the fence, team 2 was standing back to back firing at the two separate hordes coming at them from different directions. As the team fought, Bryar looked over at the group running out of the facility doors.

"Rodriguez! Fucking help us!" he ordered, clearly not noticing the 15 extra people running out of the building. Where the Lieutenant should have remained confident and calm, he sounded like a small child panicking. John would admit the experience would terrify anyone, this was no excuse. The Lieutenant always sounded like this in the face of actually having to see combat.

"Don't stand your ground! Get to the damn trucks!" John shouted back to Bryar.

Miller, Rookie and the other 2 soldiers ran towards the trucks and laid down covering fire as the civilians loaded into the back of the troop carrier. John began to run after them and stopped as he watched in horror as the beasts began to overrun team 2.

The sniper who was posted in the trees now sat above the rippling bridge. He fired his MK14 into the oncoming creatures but it wasn't enough. A few rounds punched through the beasts but several of them climbed quickly up the tree and threw him out of it. He screamed as his limbless body, still alive, was thrown 10 feet outward onto the top of the razor wire fence and stuck there as he was electrocuted to death.

"Jesus Christ! Take them down!" another man in team 2 screamed at the sight. John was about to run to their aid when behind him, the horde giving chase had burst through the front facility entrance. They were now coming from 3 directions.

"Holy fuck! 6 'o' clock!" yelled another man as he turned to fire at the horde. The beasts were closing in fast from all directions.

"Get out of there!" yelled John to the men.

"He's right! Fuck this!" yelled a man John recognized as Corporal Walt. He turned and ran towards the truck, tailed by Private Alan.

As the two men ran to the trucks, the swarm caught up to the others. One man was dragged to the ground and pulled into the woods screaming in horror. He could be heard crying for dear life in the brush as he was being eaten alive. Bryar and the other man turned and ran.

"Get those vehicles fired up and ready to move!" John yelled to Miller and Rookie. The two men, and the other soldiers jumped into the troop carrier and 2 trucks as soon as Walt and Alan got to them.

"Get the civilians out of here! We can handle ourselves" Miller yelled to Rookie who jumped in the driver's seat of the transport full of civilians and drove off, away from the facility with a truck of soldiers following. John ran for the last truck as Miller and Pots provided covering fire from the doors.

John ran as fast as he could but out of nowhere he was tackled to the ground by one of the beasts. He got back to his feet quickly and kept running but was tackled by another. He tried to climb back up but was dragged back to the ground. He kicked with all of his strength at the beasts, breaking the nose of the one holding his ankle, but it did no good. He felt a claw slice through his skin and blood spilled onto the green grass. He screamed in pain but continued to fight. He reached for his pistol but it had been kicked away by one of the beasts. He drew his knife and plunged it through the wrist of the beast holding him, pinning its arm to the ground. He crawled away, and was grabbed by another beast, with another one stomping on his ribs. He felt one of them crack and coughed as the air was knocked from his lungs. This was it. He had escaped the last near death incident but wouldn't this time. His vision began to blacken and he saw stars.

"Get the hell off of him!" he heard Pots yell as he tackled the beast above him to the ground, setting John free. He gasped as he struggled for air and painfully filled his lungs. Miller ran up to him and threw him around his shoulder, helping him to his feet.

"Get him to the truck!" Pots yelled as he stood back up firing his rifle.

John glanced back at his brother as Miller dragged him toward the truck. Pots stood in the open, facing the oncoming horde, firing as he walked backwards.

Miller threw John into the backseat and turned to shoot. To the other side of the car John saw Bryar and one of his men sprinting toward them screaming.

"Don't leave! I don't want to die!" Bryar yelled, crying. As he did this one of the beasts tackled his man to the ground and the swarm overtook him. "God, please don't leave me!" Bryar continued to scream.

From the backseat John fired a spare rifle he had found lying across the back dashboard at the horde chasing Bryar while Miller covered Pots' escape. As Bryar reached the truck, one of the creatures reached out and grabbed his back with both clawed hands and dragged down hard. Bryar screamed in agony. John aimed his rifle at the creature and blew its head off of its body as Bryar climbed into the vehicle and toppled over, lying across John's lap.

"I-I'm s-s-sorry." Bryar said before letting out a long, final breath. John looked down at the Lieutenants' back and saw the beast had stripped it of all flesh and meat, leaving his spine as well as his ribs exposed. Blood pooled on the floor of the black truck. Bryar the coward was dead. The swarm continued to close in around them.

"Go!" yelled Pots to Miller as he was grabbed and pulled backwards by a beast. "Get the fuck out of here!"

"Fuck!" Miller yelled as he turned and jumped into the driver's seat.

"No! No! Go back! We can't leave him!" John yelled at Miller, fighting to get out of the moving vehicle as Miller drove away. Bryars heavy body on top of him made this difficult.

"There's too many! We have to go! I'm sorry!" Miller yelled back to John.

"No! We can't! We have to-" John said as he was cut off by Pots speaking quickly over local coms. He sounded to be in extreme pain and breathed heavily as he was being dragged down.

"Get out John. Live your life. This was for you. I love you brother." Pots said as he was dragged into a pile of drooling beasts. He screamed over the coms as several mouths gnawed on his flesh. "End this shit! Pots out!" he cried into the coms followed by white noise.

"No! No! God dammit no!" John yelled, tears streaming down his face. He looked back at the facility behind them fading away and saw nothing but smoke and grey flesh swarming the area. As they drove away they saw the blue bridge flash and disappear. The battle was over and the bridge had closed; but more were soon to come.

As John sat in the back of the truck sobbing, he heard Miller breathing heavily in the front seat trying not to succumb to insanity from what he had seen today and before coming through the bridge.

"I'm sorry. Im so fucking sorry. I brought this. I'm so sorry." Miller said while driving, his voice shaking. "I didn't mean for this to happen."

The men sat in silence for a few minutes taking in the past events before the radio in the truck came to life.

"Fort Hodge command to QRF, report immediately your situation. What the hell is going on?" the voice of the radio operator said, eager for a report. Several seconds of silence passed before the voice spoke again. "Drones show a fucking warzone at Facility 12. What the hell happened? Someone report? Lieutenant Bryar, do you copy?"

John was still in shock from losing his brother moments ago and couldn't speak. Seconds more passed by before he heard the voice of Rookie over the radio in the transport.

"QRF to Fort Hodge. On our way back now. It's a fucking shitshow, sir. Civilians and wounded being transported. Multiple casualties."

"Son, where is Lieutenant Bryar?" the radio operator said.

"Dead, sir." Rookie replied. Several seconds passed before the response came through.

"The Colonel wants a full briefing when you're back. We await your return. Son, he is not happy and he wants some answers." At this comment, John finally came back to life and grabbed the radio and spoke.

"I think we all do"

<u>SEVEN</u>

2nd Lieutenant Steve Miller sat behind the wheel of the truck, speeding down the dirt road to catch up to the other 2 vehicles ahead of them. He looked in the rear view mirror and saw the facility had disappeared from view and all that was visible was trees and the dust the truck was kicking up from the road. In the backseat, Staff Sergeant Rodriguez sat crying, covered in blood and wounded with his dead leader laying across his lap. Rodriguez had been silent for 5 minutes now; the only audible sound being his occasional sniffle. The man was in shock from his loss and Miller knew exactly how he felt. Before entering this new dimension, Miller had seen hell and what it brought. He had seen things he wanted to forget but couldn't. He had lost so many people that were constantly popping up in his mind. He couldn't escape the nightmare that was his own memory. He was haunted by his thoughts, and there was no escape from it. He sat behind the wheel of the truck as he reached the rest of the convoy and thought about the events leading up to the bridge.

He remembered the day it started; the day his perfect life came crumbling down around him. Steve Miller was a veteran of the United States Marine Corps. He had served his time over the course of many years all for his country. He had seen all sorts of different terrains. From deserts to mountains, he had seen it all. Being a long term soldier for marine recon was a tough job, but he was a tough man. Finally, after years upon years of experience, he finally had decided to retire. Back home he had it all. A wife, 2 young daughters, and a beautiful place in southern California that he could proudly call home. Just like in this new dimension, a deadly plague had wiped out a significant portion of humanity, but he was lucky enough to make it out of it all unscathed. His family was entirely intact and that's all that mattered to him. He lived the perfect life and he wouldn't trade it for anything. He missed those days, and the thought of it brought a tear to his eye. All it took was 14 days for his life and the world he knew to come crashing down around him.

It was a Wednesday morning in what most people would consider a beautiful July. The month had been nothing but sunny and warm. To most people this was absolutely lovely but to Miller, it was sort of uncomfortable. He preferred the cold, but his wife loved the area so he stayed. He didn't mind making his family happy. A small sacrifice to make for all that they had sacrificed over the years for his military career.

The family was outside in the backyard. The kids were playing with the dog while he and his wife sat on the porch enjoying the scene. Miller had been retired from the military for a week now and couldn't be happier. The day was perfect up until it wasn't. Sudden sirens sounded from the firehouse. Announcements came over the radio and television all saying the same thing.

"NASA reports saying a group of meteors are to strike earth within the next hour. Expect heavy destruction and casualties. If you have a safe shelter, take to it immediately. Do not be caught out in this event. Listen to local emergency officials and the radio broadcasts for further updates."

Miller had never heard of a natural disaster of meteor strikes before. At first he was excited, but the more he thought about it the more worried he became. If the government was making a broadcast about the event as a warning, this would be bad. He and his wife quickly got the girls together, grabbed the dog, some water and food, and headed to the basement. It seemed as soon as they shut the basement door, things started to kick off.

Outside all that they heard was crashing and explosions. The ground shook with each impact. Above them, Miller heard one of the rocks smash through their upstairs, crumbling half of the house above them. The girls were crying, his wife was trying to comfort them. The scene was complete and utter chaos. After about 20 minutes however, the impacts stopped. Silence took over. Fire sirens began to sound outside as emergency services began to assist those in need. Miller turned on the radio and listened.

"Impacts have occurred globally. At this time we aren't completely sure of the death toll, but we can assume it to be in the high millions. Destruction is widespread and extreme. If you or anyone else is injured, please reach out to your local emergency response teams immediately."

Miller and his family had left the basement and went outside. The destruction they witnessed was mind blowing. Fire and chunks of debris lay all around them. No buildings were left untouched, including their own home. Fire trucks, ambulances and police cars (that were left undestroyed) drove around assisting the wounded. The scene was gruesome. At the time, that was the most disturbing thing that Miller had ever seen. After leaving the safety of their basement, the family was taken to a FEMA camp by a National Guard evacuation where they would wait to hear further news. The camp filled fast. Civilians were taken care of while those who were able to help with what they could, did. The Miller family spent 6 days there, and in those 6 days they began to hear strange rumors.

"People are sick!"

"Could it be the virus again?"

"No, it's new. It came with those asteroids!" This was one conversation that Miller had overheard from the National Guard soldiers one morning.

"Reports from the heavily inflicted zones say people are devouring one another. Like some sort of fucking cannibals, man. And there are these worms. The asteroids are full of the little fuckers. Alien worms or some shit, man."

"I heard about this. These worms or parasites or whatever the fuck they are. They are like, taking control of people or some shit. It's wild, bro."

At the time this was thought to be a rumor, but over the course of the next few days this was proven to be true. All over the globe people were beginning to cannibalize each other. And it wasn't just the people. Animals were becoming bloodthirsty as well, all of which stemmed from the presence of these small alien worms from within the meteors. They would burrow into a host and take control of them, using them to feed on any form of fresh meat that they could find. Humans and animals alike were on the menu. By the time it had been 1 week since the meteors fell, the world was experiencing a full biological pandemic. These infected, parasitized beings were overrunning cities and shelters, devouring and further tormenting those who were unfortunate enough to be in their way. The worms were everywhere as well, looking for suitable hosts to control. The world was in a full panic. Full military forces were deployed and a draft was reinstated to gather a fighting force to stop the onslaught of humanity. Miller was called back to service.

For days, battles raged against the growing threat; but loss after loss made it clear humanity was seeing its last days. Miller had seen city after city fall. Chicago, New York, Atlanta. There was no stopping these things, especially once the wildlife were infected as well; and as time went on, the creatures became deadlier. Whereas the freshly infected beings were originally blood thirsty versions of themselves, they now were mutating and evolving. It only took a matter of days for it to happen, but once infected, the worms would mutate the host into becoming a more deadly killer. Humans lost pigmentation to develop a natural camouflage blending with the urban environment and battlefields. They grew claws, became more agile, and strong. They also developed pointed teeth and wide mouths for more efficient feeding. While resembling their former selves by keeping traits like hair and height, these creatures were mostly unrecognizable as being human. Mutations happened with animals as well. Some predators would grow in size or develop more deadly traits. The perfect world that Steve Miller had once lived became a horror show within days. By the 11th day since the meteor strikes, every government in the world had fallen and most of humanity was destroyed.

The few humans who remained were either in hiding, soon to be found by the efficient hunters, or were being protected by the final bastions of soldiers who remained. After losing the battle for Albany, New York, Miller had relocated his family to Fort Hodge along with the rest of his platoon and what they believed to be the last of humanity. Fort Hodge was a final safe haven for humanity. 62 civilians resided there along with 50 soldiers and about 12 support staff. Humanities days were numbered. By the 14th day, Fort Hodge had seen siege after siege and the idea occurred to use the resources at Facility 12. It was a last ditch effort to save those who remained. The idea to take refuge in another dimension was insane, but they were desperate. Miller would do anything to save his family.

A convoy of those who remained made the trip to Facility 12 which was being defended by several troops who had set up a forward operating base there. Sandbag walls were set up around the perimeter with machine guns and razor wire. Snipers were all over the roof with turrets. Humvees patrolled the area with .50 caliber machine guns. It wasn't enough. As the convoy reached the facility, they were ambushed. Thousands of beasts came out of the trees and swarmed the vehicles. Only 3 trucks made it to the facility gate while the rest of humanity was devoured. Inside the facility, the scientists worked to open the bridge but awaited permission from the other side. Miller had moved his family and the civilians into the lab while a battle raged outside. Miller remembered the sounds of screams of troops making a final defense and the children crying.

"They are through the defenses! We need to hold them back!" Miller remembered an enlisted man from the air force yelling. The facility was full of a mix of people and military personnel desperate to survive. Miller had kissed his family and assured them that he would be right back as he went with the Airman to hold the front entrance. He and many other military personnel held the doors as long as they could before the beasts burst through. It was chaos. Miller remembered his family running to him scared from the lab. He had told them to stay but they didn't. He should have stayed with them but he didn't. He remembered a giant infected man bursting through the door and killing his family. The beast slashed his daughters open with its massive claws, killing them and staining the walls with their blood. He remembered watching in horror as the 7 foot tall beast lifted his wife by the throat and crushed her neck with its hand. He remembered screaming in agony watching his family die, defenseless. He had slashed it from shoulder to hip diagonally with his bowie knife and stabbed it in the eye when it grabbed him, but it didn't kill the thing. He managed to get away and ran. He didn't remember how or why he got away but he did. One of his biggest regrets was not killing the thing and avenging his family. He got in the lab and barricaded the door as the bridge opened and he ran through, leading those who remained to safety.

The memory haunted Miller. It had only been a couple hours ago he had lost his family so he understood exactly how Staff Sergeant Rodriguez felt at this moment. They were in the same boat. To make things worse, Miller wanted to die. He had hoped for death but he couldn't die yet. When he had set off from Fort Hodge he had one mission, to save those who remained of humanity. He couldn't save his family but he would be damned if these others had to die as well and now that he had opened the bridge to another dimension, he had brought the bane of humanity with him on his trail. He blamed himself for this mess and feared he had doomed this dimension. He couldn't stop fighting till his people were safe and the bridge was closed. He wouldn't stop. When his mission was completed, then he could die.

As he thought to himself in his fits of post-traumatic stress flashbacks, Rookie filled in command over the radio on the situation further. Command was eager to learn more and didn't understand the new threat facing them. Miller had not paid any attention to what was going on and just drove.

"QRF, you are approaching Fort Hodge. We can see you. Opening gates now." said the radio operator through the speakers, anticipation present in his voice.

Miller snapped back to reality and looked ahead at the monstrous fort. 3 rows of chain link fences topped with electric razor wire surrounded the concrete walls that encircled the base. Sniper nests and machine gun towers topped the walls. Bunkers and armed Humvees sat on either side of the front gate, which creaked open slowly to let the convoy in. The gunners of the fort focused their aim on the vehicles the entire way in. Behind them the gates slammed shut and the convoy came to a halt inside the walls. All around them troops clad in black tactical gear surrounded the vehicles with their guns aimed at them.

"Remain calm and put your weapons down. Per precaution, Fort Hodge command has authorized lethal force if necessary, but we don't want it to come to that." a Major said from behind a row of soldiers. "My name is Major LeBlanc, United States Army, second in command here. We just need to examine you and learn what is going on. Please, peacefully step forward."

All of the people exited the trucks and stood in a line in front of the firing squads. The Major continued.

"Now will all of the 'others' step forward for questioning."

"Others? What do you mean by others?" Rookie asked, confused.

"People from the other end of the bridge. The others. They need to be processed before being released to the fort." LeBlanc said.

Miller, his remaining soldiers, and the civilians all stepped forward.

"Who is in charge here?" asked LeBlanc.

Miller stepped forward from the line.

"That would be me." Miller said.

"Great. Sergeant, have your men cuff this man and the others and lock the others up." LeBlanc ordered one of his men.

"What the hell? You can't do that! These are innocent people!" Rookie exclaimed, forgetting his place. Miller just sat in awe, not expecting to be taken captive after escaping near death.

"The Colonel wants the leader for questioning, Private. Stand back and keep your mouth shut!" LeBlanc replied to Rookie's outburst.

"These are people!" Rookie yelled.

Suddenly from behind LeBlanc and all of his men Miller heard a deep, disgusted voice speak with a hint of a southern drawl. "That's for me to decide."

Colonel Hodge.

<u>EIGHT</u>

Colonel Hodge walked out from behind his line of troops who had the 'others' handcuffed and at gunpoint, including the little girl that was in the group. He slowly walked in front of them, examining each one closely and then turned to his Major.

"Major LeBlanc, I want you to see to it that the QRF team is inspected for contagion and held under quarantine till we figure out what the hell happened up at Facility 12." he said in his deep, southern drawl. Then he turned and looked over the 'others' again. "I want these-" he paused "-these things, locked up while I question their leader."

"Colonel, these are people! You can't treat them like this! They are just trying to get to safety!" Rookie exclaimed, yet again forgetting his lack of rank. The Colonel turned to face the young man.

"Son, I don't know who the fuck you think you are talking to, but I am going to make it simple for you. 1, I am in charge of this fort. 2, I will decide if they are or are not people. They don't even belong to this dimension. They don't technically exist! And 3, if you speak out of line one more time I will have your sorry ass court marshaled and locked up. Am I clear?" Hodge stared Rookie down intensely, fire burning in his eyes. He was enraged at the loss of his facility.

"Clear sir." Rookie sighed, realizing his mistake.

"Good." he turned back to LeBlanc. "Major, I want you to bring the leader and Doctor Allen to my office for questioning immediately. We will figure out what the fuck exactly happened to my facility."

"Sir, some of the QRF team are wounded. Shall we treat their wounds before quarantining?" LeBlanc asked cautiously.

Hodge stopped and thought about the question. He then replied arrogantly, "I do believe that Corporal Walt is a trained field medic?"

"That's correct, sir." Walt replied.

"Then have him patch them up. Why waste precious resources on the men that fucked up my high tech facility." Hodge said in spite as he walked away towards the main command building.

Everyone, including the Major, stood in awe at the comment.

"Did I fucking stutter on my orders, Major? Get these people moving!" The Colonel said before slamming the door to the building.

"Sergeant, take the others to lock up and quarantine QRF there as well till further orders are given." LeBlanc said quietly. One of the soldiers in black followed by some of his men rounded up the QRF team. LeBlanc stopped the group before they could be taken away.

"You," he said pointing at Miller. "You and Doctor Allen come with me."

—

"Sorry, Rodriguez." Walt said to John as he winced in pain from the medical attention Walt was providing. The gash down John's right calf muscle was so deep that it required stitches, and thanks to the hospitality of Hodge, Walt wasn't given anything to numb the wound. Every pull of the needle brought pain.

The 4 remaining men from the QRF had been locked up in the cells beneath the barracks for 5 hours now, waiting for any word on their release.

"Don't apologize to me, man." said John. "It's that fucker Hodge that put us in this situation."

Colonel Hodge was a cruel man, but well known throughout the United States Army. Originally serving in Vietnam, he gained his power and respect from missions he and his team had completed in the field when he was just a Captain. During the war, Hodge had been recognized for his leadership and bravery completing these missions, but rumor had it that Hodge hadn't done shit. Just like Bryar, Hodge enjoyed sitting back and sending his well-trained men to die while he took credit for their success. With Hodge being Bryar's grandfather, it made sense that the two men were so much alike in their leadership. Their relationship was the whole reason Bryar ended up with an officer's rank at Fort Hodge. The men were very similar except where as Bryar was a pussy, Hodge was just a careless asshole and it showed. Bryar's death as well as the loss of Facility 12 had triggered Hodge to act crazier than he already was. A dangerous mental state for a man with his own personal guard and secret fort.

"What do you think he is gonna do with us? I mean he can't do this, can he? There has to be some sort of rules." Rookie said, angry at the situation.

"Yea and who are you gonna tell, Rookie? You're a Private, and locked down here." Alan said laughing at the new addition to their team. Rookie looked down at the ground trying to hide his embarrassment.

"Shit man, you had a hell of a first mission today, huh?" Walt said.

"I don't think I'm ever going to sleep again." replied Rookie, shuttering at the thought. He continued to himself saying the names of the deceased. "Zebra, Bryar, Pots-"

"Pots isn't fucking dead." John snapped. He was still in shock and had not accepted his friend was dead yet.

"What? I thought he got-" Rookie started before he was cut off by Walt.

"Rookie, shut the fuck up." Walt snapped, giving the rookie a look.

"Pots isn't dead. He was right there. He was right there and he just-" John was saying to himself, and began shaking, his eyes swelling with tears.

"Shhh. It's okay man. If you say Pots aint dead, he aint dead." Walt said, trying to calm the shocked man. As Walt spoke, he snipped off the end of the thread, finishing up the stitches he was giving.

"Shit, I'm sorry man." Rookie said regretfully.

"It's okay, because Pots ain't dead. He just ain't here." Walt said quietly and kindly to Rookie, motioning his head towards John.

John sat silently breathing, calmed down, took a deep breath and said to his men, "No. Your right. Pots is gone. He is gone. He saved me." He took another deep breath and looked around the room at the pitiful gazes of his men who had known the two were like family. "He's gone, but we aren't. And we are going to end this. We are going to make Pots proud."

—

Miller sat furious in Hodge's office next to Dr. Allen as the two men were handcuffed to their chairs in front of Hodge's desk.

"You really expect me to believe this sci-fi shit?" Hodge said chuckling in an arrogant tone. "This is some shit out of a horror movie! Alien parasites turning people into beasts? Bridges opening wild all over the world? Bridges that you yourself created, Doctor. How stupid do you think I am?"

"Is it any crazier than dimensional travel, sir? The project at Facility 12 was your own program, you should know anything is possible." Allen replied, a little baffled by Hodge's disbelief.

"It sounds like you are trying to question my intelligence, Doctor? I really hope that you aren't for your sake." Hodge said sternly with a straight face. The man's wrinkled face showed anger, as his thick grey eyebrows curved inward below his groomed, short, grey hair.

"Sir, I am not a soldier. You can't just-" Allen started before being cut off.

"I can't just what? Lock you up for destroying my expensive facility? I thought hiring the top graduate of MIT would lead to great things, but instead I am faced with the death of my grandson and the loss of my facility thanks to you two fuck ups!" Hodge yelled, standing up from his chair behind his wooden desk.

"Don't listen to this prick, Doctor." said Miller.

"You better watch your goddamn tone, son." Hodge snapped at Miller. "You're pretty bold for a man who doesn't exist."

"Are you stupid or something?" Miller said laughing. It was obvious he existed. He was here. Hodge was just desperate to be in control of what he did not understand. Hodge did not like that and met the man's laughter with a slap to the side of the head.

"Don't. Fuck. With. Me." Hodge said, getting close to Miller's face. "If it were up to me I would line up all of you-you- whatever you are, and blast you all out of existence! But unfortunately word of your existence has reached General McCalister, so until he arrives, I have to keep you alive."

Miller spread a cocky grin and replied, "Oh, so now I exist."

Realizing his poor choice in words, Hodge made a fist and bashed Miller in the face, breaking his nose. Blood streamed down Miller's lips and his face throbbed but he started laughing.

"You really have something to prove, don't you?" Miller said.

"Until you start telling me the truth, I will continue to treat you like the vermin you are!" Hodge yelled. "Feeding me this shit about parasites and 'bridge events' is making me very impatient!"

"Sir, he isn't lying! The fabric of our dimension is unstable! We need to alert the world of these bridge events soon before the events spread!" Allen exclaimed. "And when these events spread, so will these creatures!"

"Okay Doctor, please entertain me. If this event is happening then why are we not receiving reports?" Hodge said.

"I think it has something to do with the arc." Allen replied. Hodge looked confused and impatient.

"English doctor." Hodge said. Miller chuckled. He wasn't a scientist and even he understood Allen. Hodge was just dense.

"The ring that harnessed the energy for the bridge. When it was destroyed, the bridge was open. By destroying the arc, the harnessing power was destroyed making our fabric unstable. These things will open and close on their own now. I think that we should expect the bridges to open more near the site of the arc where the original energy was drawn to, and then slowly work its way outward." Allen said, speaking slowly for the Colonel.

"Okay Doctor. And if this is the case, why aren't we seeing it anywhere else?" Hodge chuckled arrogantly.

"Dumb ass, he just told you! It's not going to be instantaneous! You need to put out a word, now! We need to form a plan!" Miller yelled, having officially lost his patience. This time Hodge called in LeBlanc.

"Major, I want this abomination removed from my office and thrown in a cell with the other, filth!" Hodge ordered.

"You're making a mistake! You're going to get people killed!" Miller yelled as he was dragged out of the room.

"We will see about that. I don't like fairy tales, and I'm not about to play your game."

Just as Miller was being dragged out of the room and Hodge sat down in his chair, a Corporal from the fort's communication staff ran into the room and threw up a salute.

"Colonel, sir. We have a problem." the young Corporal said quickly.

"We don't have all day, Corporal. Spit it out." the Colonel said, clearly annoyed that the young soldier interrupted his meeting.

"There's a situation happening in Syracuse, New York. It's- well its-" the Corporal stuttered.

"Well, what is it?" Hodge said, annoyed.

"Well sir, I don't know how to explain it. But it looks like a bridge."

Miller glared at Hodge, knowing what was about to await the small city in upstate New York. Hodge took a step back, baffled by the realization the Doctor had been telling the truth, but he wouldn't admit that. The man cared more about his pride than other people.

"Oh my. It's happening." Allen said, shocked.

"You need to deploy forces now, Colonel! Evacuate the city!" Miller yelled.

"LeBlanc! Didn't I tell you to get this thing out of here!" Hodge yelled at his second in command, throwing the stapler that sat on his desk at the door.

"Yes sir" LeBlanc said as he continued to pull Miller away.

"Sir, the governor has the National Guard on the way. Should we send assistance?" the Corporal said.

"Colonel, please." Allen pleaded. "Warn the troops about what they will face. Warn somebody, please!"

"Let's see how this plays out first. I have faith that those troops will see this through." Hodge said, turning his back to Allen.

"God help them." Allen said.

<u>NINE</u>

Jessica Richmond had been leaving her job at the hospital after a long night shift of 12 hours. It was now 9 o'clock in the morning and she was more than ready to head home after the crazy night that she had just had. Most of her night of nursing was spent tending to people who she had basically thought to be insane. It had been a year and a half since the outbreak that ravaged the globe had disappeared, and its results still lurked about. Jessica had seen the news reports of cults out west driving people to insanity and terrorizing the nation. What they were doing was sick, but the spread of insanity wasn't just limited to the west. Even in the northeast people had been resorting to crazy things. Some people turned violent, just trying to find a place to put their anger. Some people were worse than violent.

One of Jessica's patients of the night was a middle aged man who had seemed to lose all sense of reality. Just like the cultists out west, he had resorted to an extreme take on his religious beliefs. The man had believed that he was a messenger of god, sent to earth to spread word of a coming plague. This was a common theme among these religious nuts. Although completely and utterly crazy, that was not why he was in the hospital. The man had taken a razor blade to himself and carved a deep cross across his entire chest, claiming it as his sacrifice of flesh to the lord. His neighbor had found him bleeding out in the hallway outside of his apartment and called an ambulance. The man didn't regret his actions and was even angry at the hospital staff for trying to help him, claiming it was not the will of the lord. When Jessica had tried to disinfect the wound, the man lashed out and tried to strike her. One of the security staff at the hospital had to cuff the man to his bed and stand guard.

It was not unusual for there to be armed security guards in the hospital. After the world went to shit and people went crazy, it was deemed necessary to keep the hospitals safe. 8 security staff were hired to patrol the hospital at all times, protecting the staff from unruly patients, and possible threats of terrorism. So far, not many attempts from the insane terrorist cult, The Chosen, had reached New York State, but with the pace that they were growing, that would soon change and they needed to be ready. The nation was headed down a path of violence that would soon escalate further; at least that's what Jessica had heard on the news when watching television. "One day at a time." she would tell herself every morning. There were already crazy people here and she didn't need to worry about more.

Jessica walked out of the hospital in downtown Syracuse into the cool, July morning air. It was a sunny day of about 66 degrees Fahrenheit so far, and was looking to get warmer. Even though the world was slowly going to shit, she didn't let it distract her from the fact that today was a beautiful day. She looked out to the street in front of her. It was busy with traffic and people headed to and from work. Many of these people still wore face masks out of fear that the virus that killed so many in the past would soon return. Jessica often had fears of this herself but tried to not let it bother her. She walked down the sidewalk to her vehicle that was parked on the street. She had to squint to look through the warm sunlight that shined on her long brown hair. All around her, life went on, and she thought about the virus. Humanity was strong and could get through anything, she thought. The virus had wiped out a huge portion of humanity and she had been on the frontlines of the disease prevention effort, working in the medical field. She knew humanity's strength better than anyone. She took one final glance around her and smiled; not because of the virus but because of how hardy humans were. Sure, maybe the world was going to shit, but as she looked around she realized two things- humans were strong, and humans were everywhere.

Jessica got into her car and pulled away from the curb outside of the hospital that she had worked so hard at. She had been a nurse for 3 years now and learned so much about herself. She never had realized how much she actually enjoyed helping those in need, and she never realized how brave she was when faced with a difficult situation. Her hardiness was most likely what got her through the crazy times of the pandemic. She was proud of herself, but not as proud as her husband had been. Her husband had stood by her side through all of the hard times, and supported every decision she had made with her career. Even after she had accidentally brought home the virus and gotten him sick, he stood by her. She had been lucky enough to be asymptomatic and not receive any of the nasty symptoms, but her husband had not been so lucky. She watched him die in quarantine as he seized uncontrollably till death. Right before he passed away, she remembered him placing his hand on the glass barrier separating them and told her, "I love you. It's not your fault. Make me proud." Those were his last words before dying. For months she had been a train wreck. She continued to sulk in sorrow but she had to move on. That's what he would have wanted. His final request was to make him proud and from that day on that's what she continued to do. The entire experience was what drove her to be such an outstanding nurse.

Jessica drove down the street to the main intersection outside of the hospital where she met a red light. She slowed her car as she eased her foot on the brakes and looked around. At first glance you would never guess an eighth of humanity had been killed not too long ago. The streets were packed.

The light turned green and a car beeped from behind her and she drove forward. Her eyes were heavy as she drove. She couldn't wait to go to bed. The downside of working so hard was that she was constantly tired. She blinked away the urge to sleep and kept on driving. She rounded the corner of a building, driving under an overpass and stopped. The sight ahead of her was very strange, and any wish to sleep had been shocked out of her. She put her car in park and sat straight up in her seat.

Ahead of her was a long line of vehicles in a traffic jam, with crowds of hundreds of people stepping out of their vehicles or running from down the street to the front of the jam. Police had the road blocked off and had armed officers directing people away from the area. Confused as to what was going on, Jessica, too, found herself leaving her vehicle to join the crowd. She walked at a fast pace along with hundreds of other people up towards the police barricade.

"Does anyone know what is going on?" someone next to her said.

"Is it another riot? A protest maybe?" said another.

Jessica moved further up the group towards the blockade that the police had set up. She looked off to the left between buildings and noticed that the other road parallel to this one was also blocked off and filled with curious civilians. The sounds of sirens filled the air as more police cars whirled into the area off of the ramp to the highway, and parked, blocking traffic from entering from there as well.

"Something doesn't feel right about this." said a chubby, balding man in a suit. He turned, noticing Jessica's scrubs and work ID tag he asked, "Hey do you know what's going on? You public servants are all buddy buddy aren't you?"

Jessica shook her head at the stupid comment and replied, "I can't exactly say I am in with the Syracuse police department. I am a nurse."

"Well that's not very helpful" the chubby man said as he worked his way to the front of the pack. This was probably the fastest that he had ever moved, Jessica had assumed.

As Jessica neared the front, she began to see a bright blue light glowing over all of the vehicles behind the barricade. The light shimmered like light shining through an aquarium of water, but she couldn't see where it was coming from.

"Please remain in your vehicles. Remove yourself from the area in a calm and orderly fashion." a police officer standing at the front of the barricade was saying into a megaphone. He kept repeating the statement, but people continued to push forward. "This area has been locked down for your own safety. Please remove yourself from the area." He continued.

Overhead a news helicopter flew just above the buildings. The number 5 showed on the side of the chopper. At least if Jessica couldn't see what was going on here, the news channel she watched would.

At the front of the barricade, a news crew with a cameraman was arguing with the officers who refused to let them in.

"It's not safe to enter. As of right now we do not know what is going on." an officer repeated to the camera crew.

"We have our rights to freedom of press!" yelled the news anchor.

"You do, just not within a locked down zone." the officer calmly replied.

Jessica had finally reached the front of the barricade where the shimmering light was the brightest and was taken aback. To the left, around the corner of a building she saw a large, blue, shimmering oval hovering just above the ground's surface. It rippled blue waves across it, almost like it was vertically standing water. The blue color shimmered, changing from light to dark blue constantly, putting off the bright glow that covered everything around it.

"What the fuck." Jessica muttered to herself.

"I think i've seen that before!" yelled a woman to her right. "Yeah! I have definitely seen this on TV!"

"Isn't that one of those things from the news that the government had made? What'd they call them again?" another man said.

"It's a bridge." Jessica said, completing the man's thought as she stared forward in amazement at the bright blue portal.

"No way. I thought they were blowing smoke up our asses." said another man to her left. Jessica remembered watching the news coverage about the bridge a couple weeks ago on TV. They interviewed a government scientist who made this discovery. Doctor Allen? She thought that was the man's name. He had preached about a new found peace for mankind to unite under and scientific breakthroughs. In all honesty she didn't believe it either, even after they showed a quick clip of the open bridge. She had assumed the government would be desperate to make up some story to make the people unite after the months of rioting that had been going on all over the nation.

"This looks real enough to me man. What is it doing here?" replied another person behind Jessica. This was a question that everyone had.

"Please stay behind the police blockade!" yelled an officer in riot gear, raising his shield to the yelling crowd.

"It's here! It's finally here! The coming of times! Judgement day!" yelled a homeless man who was laughing. The man had a crazed look in his eye. Clearly he was one of the religious nuts Jessica had seen far too much of.

"Be quiet you paranoid nut!" yelled a man, throwing trash at the religious man. What looked like a paper plate covered in pizza sauce caught the man in the side of his face, splattering his scarred face and grey beard with red. The man wiped the sauce off and turned to face the crowd.

"You are all sinners! You all will see!" he screamed pointing in their faces.

"Fuck off you crazy bastard!" someone yelled as they shoved him. Another person joined in. More people began to defend the crazy man and before Jessica knew it, a mosh pit had formed in front of the police barricade.

"Break it up! Calm down!" yelled an officer as he and several others in riot gear pulled people off one another.

"Fuck this shit! I wanna see what that is!" yelled the portly man in the suit from earlier as he hopped the barricade and ran closer to the bridge. Several people followed and before the riot police could react, people began to swarm the street from all roadblocks to get a closer look at the bridge.

"Get back! Get back!" yelled an officer as he was shoved to the ground by a large man. As chaos erupted, looting and riots began to break out all around and the police took action.

"Get back behind the barricades!" yelled a police Captain into a megaphone as more riot police ran into the crowd, bashing the yelling group with their night sticks.

"Fuck you, pig!" yelled a man who threw a rock at the Captain, which smacked into his head knocking him over. The man was quickly taken down by a riot cop who smashed his nightstick into the man's stomach.

All around Jessica the chaos was unfolding. The city was so used to rioting that they seemed to completely forget about the giant blue portal open wide near them. Jessica ran out of the street and joined a group of people trying to avoid the violence.

"Just another day in the year 2023." one woman said as she welcomed Jessica to the safety of their group. She was right. Ever since the virus disappeared, every year following brought violence and civil unrest.

As the group turned to leave the area, they felt a feeling of a blast of air coming from the bridge. Jessica turned to face the bridge as it blasted a gust of air that took off the hat of the woman next to her. Dust and papers flew down the street, carried by the rushing air. The bridge, which before had calm waves rippling through it now looked like a raging sea. It turned a deep dark blue and began to shudder rapidly. The air gusts picked up and people began to scream. Those who were rioting stopped in their tracks, turning their attention back to the object that brought them all here to begin with. Even the police lowered their weapons and faced the anomaly. The gusts became so strong that a police car directly in front of the bridge began to rock.

"Everyone get to cover!" yelled an officer who was now concerned with the safety of the bystanders not rioting. People began to slowly walk backwards, back towards the barricades, not taking their eyes off of the bridge. Then, just as suddenly as the change in the bridge started, it stopped. All was calm again.

"What just happened? Can anyone explain this?" said a woman. Nobody answered. Everyone was silent.

Suddenly the portly man from before hopped back over the barricade and approached the bridge.

"Sir, please don't go near that!" said an officer, his voice trembling. The man blew right past the police line, but nobody dared to get close enough to the bridge to catch the man. Behind him trailed the crazy man who had started the violence moments before.

"It's so beautiful." the crazy man said, smiling as he wiped the joyful tears from his eyes. Together, he and the portly man both stood in front of the bridge. The portly man reached his hand out slowly and touched the bridge with his fingers, brushing the light blue waves.

"It's so strange. It just feels- well, I don't know. It feels cold and fluid." he said.

"Sir, please get back here!" yelled an officer from the line.

"Shut your mouth! We are experiencing a holy event. Not you or any other sinner can stop it now!" yelled the crazy man. Jessica noticed as he lifted his arms, a carving in the skin of a cross was visible just below his armpit, hanging out of his tank top. This man might as well have been one of The Chosen.

"You gotta feel this thing, man. It's like nothing else." the portly man said, sticking his hand further in. Just then the man jerked his arm back and yelped. "What the fuck was that?"

The man pulled his hand from the bridge and saw a slender, pale grey, smooth and unsegmented body of a worm about 3 inches long latched onto the underside of his wrist.

"You've been marked. You are holy. It's a sign!" yelled the crazy man next to him, staring in excitement. The portly man screamed.

"Get it off! Oh fuck get it off me!" The worm was burrowing into this arm now and quickly squirming under his skin. "What the fuck is this thing! Get it out of my arm!" The man cried as he dropped to the ground. The worm moved, completely under his skin now, deeper into his body. The bulge of the creature squirmed up his arm and to his torso, curving past his rips and to the back of his neck.

"The time is here! It's time for judgement!" yelled the crazy man.

"Help me!" screamed the man as the worm sunk into his body. He screamed a high pitched cry, but within seconds the cry began to change. What started as the obvious screams of a man in pain, turned to the high pitched squeal of an animal. The man began to shake vigorously on the ground.

"Get an EMT up here now!" yelled a police officer.

"Don't you fucking move, sinner! Let it run its course!" yelled the crazy man, now brandishing a knife.

"Drop the weapon! We don't want to hurt you!" yelled the officer, now drawing his sidearm.

Behind the crazy man, the portly man stopped shaking. He sat motionless for a couple seconds while the cop and the other man had their standoff.

"He will smite you all with the power of his holy fire!" cried the crazy man, pointing his knife towards the cops.

"Drop it now or we will be forced to fire!" yelled the terrified cop.

Just then, Jessica saw the portly man sit up quickly, and turn towards the man with the knife. Blood dribbled from the corner of his mouth and he jumped to his feet. The crazy man turned around to face the portly man and they met each other's gaze.

"Yes. The time is now. You have been chosen." the crazy man said lowering his knife and smiling crazed at the other man. He leaned in for the warm embrace of the embodiment of his beliefs; but right before he could grasp his new found friend, the portly man opened his mouth wide, and clamped down on the crazy man's ear. He sunk his teeth in, clamped hard, and tore away the piece of cartilage and flesh. The crazy man screamed in agony.

"Not me! I am a follower! I am holy!" he cried as he flopped onto his back.

The portly man, who still had the ear in his mouth, swallowed the piece of flesh whole and stepped towards his new found prey. Gun shots sounded and the portly man dropped onto his face on the blacktop.

"What the fuck did I just witness." said Jessica to herself as she watched a pair of cops move towards the body with pistols raised. Just as they did, the bridge began to go crazy again. This time was much shorter and ended with a bright flash, blinding the crowd watching the scene unfold. When Jessica got her vision back she saw tall, grey, humanoid creatures sprinting from the bridge towards the crazy man and the two officers.

"What the fuck are those things!" yelled one of the cops as his partner was tackled to the ground. One of the beasts bit down hard on the police officer's face with needle teeth and fed on him as he screamed. His partner began to open fire. The pop pop pop of his service pistol was heard as many more creatures sprinted out of the bridge. The officer turned to run but was stabbed through the back by a clawed hand and dragged backwards into the horde with the still screaming crazed man who was laying on the blacktop.

"Fire! Jesus Christ, open fire!" a police Sergeant yelled to his officers as they all turned from the crowd towards the oncoming beasts. The once beautiful blue bridge was now swarmed with an ocean of grey flesh and chomping jaws.

As the officers opened fire with their service pistols, swatted at the horde with their nightsticks, and shoved with riot shields, the people behind them turned to flee in horror. Jessica instantly turned and ran as well, not wanting to end up like the officers. Behind her all she could hear was the cries of the beasts, screams of men being eaten alive, and gun fire which quickly died out as the police line was overrun.

"We need to find some cover!" yelled a woman who was with Jessica. She thought of her car, which she had left at the traffic jam. It was too far now and there was no way to get it out of the jam.

"We need to get off the street!" yelled another man who was in their group. Jessica looked back and saw why. Among the hundreds of screaming civilians fleeing the scene were hundreds more of the creatures from the bridge, taking down people as they ran and gaining on Jessica and her group. The creatures were everywhere. They flooded the streets and some even began to climb the buildings, using their long claws as grips.

Overhead, the news channel 5 chopper flew low, just above one of the tall buildings. They were no doubt getting live footage of the event that millions of people all over the nation would now be watching. That was the place to be, thought Jessica. Off the ground and in the air. She was wrong.

Many of the beasts took notice of the whirling blades of the helicopter's propeller far above their heads. The noise was quite loud and drew their attention. A dozen of the things quickly began to scamper up the side of the building like lizards towards the helicopter, whose pilots were unaware. Jessica watched in horror as several of the creatures leapt onto the helicopter and began to beat at the windows. One beast on the front beat on the windshield while 2 others were on the side climbing inside the open doors. Jessica screamed as she watched one of the camera men be thrown from the open door and smack into the concrete below. The sound of his cracking skeleton was loud enough to be heard over the chaos around her.

The helicopter began to shake as the pilots tried to knock the creatures off so they could fly away, but as they did, another beast leapt from the top of a building into the tail rotor. Pink mist burst from the end of the chopper as the thing's body was shredded to meat, but the act had snapped the blades of the rotor off. The helicopter began to twirl, losing control and altitude, and crashed down into a crowd of screaming people in a fiery explosion. Jessica had to look away from the massive scene of death, especially after seeing children within the group. Nobody was safe from the horror show happening around her.

Jessica and her group continued to run as fast as they could to try to find safety, and ended up ducking into an alley way. Within the alley she, and the 4 people with her all hid behind dumpsters watching the mob pass by. At first it was all screaming people running, but then as a few seconds passed by they saw that there were creatures mixed in with the mob, tearing people apart and dragging them away; some down into the manholes in the ground.

"We can't stay here. We have to go. They will find us." said a man to Jessica and the others. His dark toned face filled with horror as he tried not to cry.

"Where is there to go? These things are everywhere!" cried a woman. Jessica pondered the question and thought of the most secure place nearby that she knew of.

"The hospital. We need to go to the hospital." she said finally.

"You're a nurse? You can get us inside?" asked the woman, eyeballing Jessica's name tag on her scrubs.

"Yes I can, but we need to move fast. More of these things are coming from everywhere." Jessica replied. "Follow me."

She led the group down the alleyway and out and around the building. Their survival was now in her hands. Most people would be panicking, but Jessica was strong. Stronger than most. Her husband's final words kept replaying through her head.

"Make me proud" she said to herself under her breath. "I will. I will make you proud."

The group continued down the street, which was now empty, the beasts mostly ahead of them giving chase to the people who had passed them by, but Jessica could hear more screaming from behind them. The bridge was still open and the creatures were hungry.

She ran quickly now, leading the group to the hospital which she could see ahead. The street was littered with gore and body remains of civilians and police officers who were not fast enough to escape. Jessica kept running towards the hospital. Ahead of them she saw a SWAT team van drive up to a building and unload a squad of tactical officers.

"There! They can protect us!" yelled a man who turned and ran to the officers waving his hands frantically.

"Get back here!" yelled a woman in a hushed voice but it was too late. From within the building they heard the screech of one of the beasts. Jessica and the rest of her group ducked behind a bus and hid from sight.

She watched as the man who had taken off running was tackled to the ground by a creature who had burst from the building window, shattering the glass. It sat on top of the screaming man swatting at his chest with its curled claws, tearing off hunk after hunk of bloody meat from his now exposed ribs. The SWAT team reacted and shot the beast off the top of the man, but as they did dozens more poured out of the building, overtaking the 6 men. Creatures waterfalled out of the office windows above the officers, engulfing the potential rescuers. Several of the men were dragged away into the building screaming. Another man had his tactical armor penetrated by the sharpened claws of a beast as it punched through his chest and into his heart. He spat blood from his mouth and hunched over. It was a slaughter, they stood no chance. Jessica had to look away and turned to her group who remained.

"We need to get to the hospital. It's our safest bet. We need to move fast and stay together!" she said, in a most commanding tone. The other people agreed and followed her.

"Make me proud." she whispered to herself again. "Make me proud."

TEN

The bridge had been open for 7 hours now in Syracuse, New York and was still dumping creatures out into the streets. It had taken 2 hours since the opening of the bridge for the National Guard first responders to arrive at the area, which could only be described as a slaughterhouse. The first wave of troops had arrived to a blood soaked feeding frenzy. Thousands of the civilians in the area had already been devoured, while thousands more were actively fleeing the city as fast as they could. The pile up of cars blocking the highways and roads had made escape by vehicle almost impossible, so evacuation attempts were slowed severely. That was where the first responding wave of troops came into play. The company of 200 Army National Guard soldiers who had formed the first wave had one job and one job only- to provide cover while civilians fled to safety. They had to hold out until reinforcements arrived. It had only taken a half an hour into entering the city to realize that reinforcements would most certainly be needed, and since there was no prior intel about what was going on or what they faced, the soldiers had no idea what to expect going into combat.

"Right side! Right side!" yelled Private Jones who had spotted the swarm of creatures quickly shifting to the right of her platoon's defensive position. They had been set up at the edge of downtown. They were the frontline platoon made up of 50 men and women who would be taking the enemy hordes head on. Behind them another platoon led the evacuation while the other two platoons guarded the flanks, farther away in the city. After fighting their way in, Jone's platoon had just enough time to set up a defensive position of several armed Humvees and some razor wire, but it wouldn't hold long. If reinforcements didn't come soon, the city would be lost.

"I want those Humvees focusing their fire on the right. Squad A, focus your fire straight ahead! Don't let them reach the wire!" yelled the Captain to her troops, who were actively firing, nearly non-stop at the oncoming waves.

As a large mass of grey flesh curved off to the right of the platoon, the gunners on the Browning M2 .50 caliber machine guns mounted to Humvees, shifted their aim with the creatures' movements. They began to open fire. Large, brass bullet casings flew through the air and pinged to the ground as the slow, deep, boom boom booms of the large guns sounded. The heavy bullets tore through the swarm, showering the streets with gore and limbs. Mixed in with this were the smaller pops of riflemen of the platoon firing bursts. Brass casings were littering the streets and the sound of the battle was deafening.

"The right side is being held back, but now they are adjusting to the left!" yelled Jones as she raised her SAW to adjust fire. She slid away from her position behind a beaten, red car and set up her rifle's bipod on the hood of a white truck to her left. Looking down her sights, she spotted the front of the new wave, sprinting at her, and pulled the trigger. The gun kicked back into her shoulder as she fired burst after burst of 5.56 NATO rounds into the horde. She counted the number of creatures she took down to herself.

"Seven, eight, nine-" she kept counting but it seemed the more she killed, the more that kept coming. To her sides, her squad also opened fire. Behind her she still heard the loud, booms, of the .50 cals.

"Fuck! They are pushing further up!" yelled a Sergeant in Jone's squad to the Captain, who stood on the hood of a car behind the group, looking through her binoculars.

"We need to hold the left! There are more bringing up the rear! Squad A and B focus fire to the left! Give them some grenades!" yelled the Captain as she lowered her binoculars and raised her M4 to fire.

Squad B moved position from the front of the defense, to the left, alongside Jones, and opened fire. Jones, quickly plucking a grenade from her tactical vest and held it firmly in her hand. She stared ahead at the thousands of oncoming beasts, pulled the pin, and threw the bomb out into the center of the horde. She watched the small, green object twirl through the air and land with a bounce onto the blacktop. Seconds later it erupted in a burst of dust, red mist, and fire. The explosion tore apart many of the creatures unlucky enough to be caught in the blast. Beside Jones, many of her squad mates followed her lead and lobbed dozens of grenades into the horde.

Multiple explosions rocked the ground around them as gore splattered the vehicles and ground.

"Left and right sides are being held, ma'am!" yelled a soldier to the Captain.

"Great! Let's hold these fuckers back till the evacuation is complete!" replied the Captain, who still stood atop the car, scanning the battlefield for changes in enemy tactics.

Jones was beginning to think optimistically about the shit situation. She had been worried for the past 7 hours about the odds of winning against these unknown things, but now she was confident in holding the enemy back. Although the waves kept coming, as long as the ammunition runs from the back kept up, they would be able to hold the enemy as long as they needed to.

"Son of a bitch." the Captain said, with dread in her voice. She had been in the back of the line trying to get a reading on the Evac situation when she received bad news. She then walked forward towards the line of her firing soldiers and passed on the news.

"Platoon Alpha to our right has been overrun! They have been radio silent for 10 minutes now, suggesting no survivors. There is now nothing stopping the enemy from circling around to our far right! I need to send a squad in that direction to cut off the advance!" She yelled out to her Platoon, with fear beginning to rise in her voice.

"How long till reinforcements arrive?" asked a fearful Sergeant from Squad C.

"ETA is unknown at this time. All I can tell you is they are on their way. There are still civilians trying to get out and until they are safe, we need to keep up the fight!" Ordered the Captain. She then turned to Master Sergeant Pratt, the leader of Jones' squad. Jones knew the order that was about to come.

"Oh god. Why me?" muttered Pratt, his voice just barely heard over the gunfire around them.

"Pratt, I need you to take Squad A and stop the enemy advance!" ordered the Captain. Sorrow filled her eyes as she knowingly commanded the troops to what would likely kill most of them; but the attempt to stop the advance was necessary for the evacuation. Pratt let out a long, sad sigh.

"Yes, ma'am. We will do our best to hold them." Pratt said.

"Good. Take one of the Humvees and move out, pronto. Godspeed, soldiers." the Captain said before turning back to the radio. Pratt slowly turned, took in the scene around him, and looked over all of his squad.

"Squad A! Let's move out!" ordered Pratt. Jones stepped away from her firing position at the hood of the truck, and followed the lead of her fellow squad mates as they ran away from the defensive position and into the city.

The squad, tailed by a Humvee, looped back behind the defensive position, avoiding the hordes rushing the rest of the platoon, and headed right into the city, abandoned by all except the creatures that wanted nothing but to feed on their flesh. The good news was that with the exception of a few wandering creatures, the streets had been empty. Jones wasn't sure if this was good or if this meant bad things were to come soon.

The squad had now been on their own traveling the streets for 20 minutes and still hadn't come across any swarms of the beasts.

"How you figure the other platoon was overrun?" asked a Private to the left of Jones, as they walked down the center of the street towards the other platoon's previously known position.

"How the hell should I know? They probably were outnumbered." stated Jones. It would only make sense. There were thousands of the creatures in the city waiting to feed.

"Yeah, okay maybe. But we were against the same odds and were holding out just fine!" the Private replied. It was a good point. The other platoon had been just as equipped and trained as they were, and they had been holding off at least 2000 before splitting away.

"Do you think the supply runs stopped coming? If so they would have run out of ammo within an hour at most." asked a Corporal, joining the conversation from behind.

"No way. The Captain would have mentioned that. Whatever happened, we need to be ready to face it ourselves." said Jones to both soldiers. Ahead of them Pratt made a shushing noise and whipped his head around to look at the 3 soldiers.

"Shut your fucking traps. I want silence. I don't know what got the other platoon but I am not trying to draw it towards us." he said shaking his head.

The entire conversation made Jones worried. The other platoon also had 50 troops and a few Humvees. Squad A had 15 personal and 1 Humvee to fight with. How were they supposed to fight off what had wiped out an entire platoon? The squad kept moving.

It had now been a half an hour and there was still no sign of a horde or the other platoon. Aside from shots in the distance and some echoing screeches, it was awkwardly quiet. They were moving down a more tightly packed, smaller street, between several buildings now when Pratt held his hand up to stop. He had seen something. Before Jones could ask what he had seen, Pratt motioned her and several others to the front of the group next to him. She quickly hurried forward.

"Did you see that, Jones?" asked Pratt.

"See what, sir?" replied Jones. She hadn't seen a thing and was too focused on watching the windows of the buildings for lurkers.

"I swear to god I just saw movement ahead of us." Pratt said pointing towards the intersection ahead. "Do you hear what I am hearing?"

Jones held her breath for a moment and listened. Nothing. The area was completely silent.

"Sir, I don't hear shit." Jones replied, confused.

"Precisely. That intersection was the last known position of Platoon Alpha before being overrun. You would think that by now we would have intercepted the enemy horde, or found survivors, but there hasn't been shit." Pratt said. He was right. The entire situation was very strange. The street was littered with brass casings and gore but that was it. In the distance, flurries of gunshots could still be heard from the other 3 platoons, reminding Jones further how odd the silence was.

"So what's the plan, sir?" Jones asked. Pratt sat quietly looking forward at the intersection before speaking.

"You, Corporal Drum, and Private Martinez are going to move up and scout out the position while we set up shop here. Those fucking beasts are going to be around here somewhere and I want to be ready." Pratt said, standing straight and holding his rifle ready. "Search for survivors and report back."

"Yes, sir." all 3 soldiers said before lining up in a tactical position and heading towards the intersection ahead.

As the soldiers crept ahead and the other platoon's defensive position came into view, Jones began to notice that things weren't adding up. All over the place there were bodies of dead creatures. Hundreds of carcasses, torn apart by gunfire, laid around the area. Limbs and guts littered the street. Jones carefully stepped over each body, checking carefully that they were in fact dead. Platoon Alpha had certainly made quite the stand here, but there was one thing missing; more like 50 things missing- Platoon Alpha. Among the bodies and destruction, not a single one of the soldiers could be found. As Jones moved further into the area, stepping over the razor wire fence with bodies toppled across it, she saw that the 3 Humvees also sat empty.

"Where the fuck are their bodies?" said Martinez, scanning the perimeter with her rifle. Jones could tell she was beginning to struggle with the mission stress.

"They must have left?" asked Drum, who was also confused. "But why wouldn't they say so?"

"Maybe the radio was trashed?" asked Jones, who was suddenly cut off by the white noise static of the radio in question. She looked around for the source and found the radio sitting between two of the Humvees, completely undamaged.

"Platoon Charlie has been overrun, we are falling back." the voice of Charlie's Lieutenant reported over the static.

"God damn. Charlie too?" said Martinez in shock.

"Well, we know one thing. They at least have a radio with them unlike these guys. Why would they leave this behind?" Jones said, curiously.

"Drum, report." said Pratt over coms to the Corporal.

"Sir, we didn't find a thing. They left their radio." Drum replied.

"Get back here. We found our missing platoon." Pratt said. The 3 soldiers turned and headed back towards the group, bringing the radio with them. When they got back they saw a most curious sight.

"There they are." exclaimed Drum, a smile on his face as he pointed at the platoon of soldiers hobbling down the street. "What the hell are they doing?"

"Soldiers! Report!" Pratt yelled down the street at the group. There was no reply.

"Where are their guns?" asked Martinez. It was a fair question. The hobbling soldiers were weaponless, just roaming the street freely.

"Hey! What the hell happened here?" Pratt yelled. "Why didn't you report?" Again there was no reply; but now the platoon turned to face the squad and moved toward them, increasing in speed.

"Drum, I think somethings wrong with them. Go check it out." Pratt said to the young medic who jogged down the road to the lost platoon. Jones watched the young soldier run up to the first man of the platoon. She was too far away to make out what was being said but suddenly the man dived on top of Drum and began to bite at his neck. Drum pushed the man's head away and yelled for help.

"What the fuck!" Pratt yelled as he and several other troops ran to restrain the crazed soldier on top of Drum. "Jones, take that radio and report we found the platoon!" While the men struggled with the crazy soldier, Jones did just that. She looked up from the radio and saw the crazed soldier bite into Drums neck, drawing an excruciating scream, gargled by the blood flooding his throat. Pratt grabbed the crazed soldier and restrained him.

"What the fuck are you doing, man!" he yelled. As he did this, the other troops from the platoon began to sprint at Pratt. He turned and as he watched, the man he was restraining bit into his hand, and tore off a finger.

"Shit! What the fuck!" he yelled as he pistol whipped the soldier to the back of the head and turned to face the oncoming platoon as Martinez tended to Drum, who was bleeding out on the blacktop.

"Stop! Hold your positions!" Jones yelled at the other platoon, but they kept coming. Suddenly, as Pratt raised his hand to the oncoming troops, one of them leapt forward and dragged him to the ground, followed by another. Together they began to claw at his eyes as he screamed. Another man dived into him and bit a piece off of his arm with a long, chewy, rip.

"What the fuck is wrong with them! Get off of him!" Martinez yelled, just as 4 more men grabbed the woman and dragged her away into a building screaming. Out of site they heard her screams intensify, with the sounds of wet lip smacking and biting.

"Jesus Christ! What do we do!" yelled another soldier as he too was tackled and had his arms ripped off by a group of the men. He let out a high pitched cry as his arms made a cringing pop as they came free from his body.

"Shit. Shit! Open fire!" yelled a Sergeant in the squad as he raised his shotgun and pumped a slug into one of the oncoming men, blasting a gaping hole through his chest.

A couple of confused soldiers ignored the order but were quickly dragged into the horde screaming. After that everyone began shooting. As the new conflict raged on, the voice of the Captain came through the radio, barely audible over the sound of the .50 cal mounted to the Humvee.

"Platoon Beta is falling back to the interstate! We are being overrun! We can't hold them much longer!" the message came as a shock. It was time to move; but this couldn't be done until they were free of these crazed soldiers.

All around Jones, her brothers and sisters in arms were dropping like flies. Some by bullet, some by brute force. It was difficult to tell who was who in this mess.

"Fall back! Fall back!" yelled a Sergeant as he walked backwards shooting. They had killed maybe 12 of the crazed men but it didn't deter the assault. Jones fell back as the Humvee was overrun. The gunner tried to climb out of the turret as he was dragged back into the hole. Blood sprayed the inside of the vehicle's windows as he was torn apart. Their main defense was gone.

"Run! Fall back to the Evac site! Radio command!" yelled the Sergeant as he was tackled into a brick wall, smashing his skull and killing him instantly.

"Command, this is Squad A of Platoon Beta, falling back! We are in pursuit by Platoon Alpha. They are going crazy, killing us!" Jones yelled into the radio. She didn't care about formality, she just wanted to know what the fuck was going on.

"Squad A, fall back to Evac. We have to hold the line until reinforcements arrive or these civilians are dead." replied the voice of the Captain.

"Shit! They are gonna kill us all!" screamed a soldier tripping in the street. He did a quick tuck and roll, losing his rifle. He came back up onto his feet, unarmed, unprotected, just to be smashed into by the horde. They needed to find a way out of the intersection fast or they would all die.

"Run into that alleyway! We will bottleneck them there!" yelled Jones to the 5 remaining troops, who all agreed from lack of options. The soldiers all ran into the alley and set up a defensive position behind some old crates that served as a slight barrier to defend. Jones once again set up her SAW on a bipod and began firing fast bursts into the horde as the other soldiers took cover. She continued her body count from earlier. "Twenty one, twenty two, twenty three." Her heart was beating out of her chest, but unlike earlier, the numbers were making a difference. As the shooting continued, less and less enemies were present. Within a few minutes, all of the crazed platoon had been killed. Jones and the 5 remaining troops stepped out from the alleyway and looked over the intersection they had just fought for. Bodies were everywhere, and it was impossible to tell who was friend and who was foe. At first glance, it would have looked like friendly fire, had Jones not been there herself.

"What the fuck just happened." said a soldier behind Jones coming out of the alley way.

Jones stayed silent. She was out of possible answers. There was no reasonable explanation for what they had just seen. Nothing topped how crazy this was. The bridge and the beasts seemed normal compared to this.

"Fuck this shit and fuck command! They sent us in with no information on what we were getting into! We just got slaughtered!" yelled another soldier. It was true, and they all were pissed, and it would be guaranteed nobody would explain this either. Just then the radio came back on.

"Squad A, where the hell are you? We need support!" yelled the Captain over the sound of heavy gunfire. Before Jones could answer, something caught her eye.

Just ahead of the remainder of the squad was a sight never seen by any of the soldiers. All over the street, creeping from the storm drains and buildings were these small, slender, grey worms. They crept closer and closer to the soldiers, squiggling all over the place.

"What the hell. This day just keeps getting weirder and weirder." said a soldier who approached the worms. He leaned down for a better look. "What are these little guys? I have never seen anything like them before."

"Who cares about worms. Let's move." said Jones, stomping on a cluster of the tiny organisms. As she did, the others all over the road seemed to react as if in pain or shock. They violently squirmed back and forth, speeding up their crawl.

"What the fuck? Get them away from me!" yelled a soldier who was stomping more into a grey paste on the sidewalk. Jones joined in and as she did, they began to crawl up her boots.

"Hey, what? Get off!" she yelled in disgust, bending down to swipe the worms off with her hand. As she did one clung onto the palm of her hand. She tried to swat it off but it stuck on, and seemed to be moving deeper, sending an excruciating pain up her arm, to her neck.

"Shit, Jones! Get that thing off you! It's like a damn leech!" yelled a soldier behind her.

"I can't!" she screamed as the pain became more violent. Blood leaked from her hand as the worm disappeared under her skin, moving as a lump up her arm. "Get it out of me! Get it out!" she cried, grabbing her knife and stabbing at the moving lump. She didn't care if she hurt herself, she wanted the pest removed. The worm cleared her shoulder and headed to the back of her neck.

"Let me get it! Sit still!" yelled a soldier, trying to hold a lighter to her skin. Jones began to spasm as the worm hit her spine and tightened. She shook uncontrollably and screamed. But her scream didn't sound like herself. It was higher pitched, and more animalistic. She didn't recognize her own voice.

"Sit still, Jones!" yelled the soldier as he now pulled a small pocket knife. "I'm gonna get that thing out!"

Before he could do anything, Jones screamed and stiff armed the man, jabbing the knife into his ribs. He gulped and dropped to his knees. Jones had no control of these spasms, and was losing control of her mind.

"Jesus Christ! Help him!" yelled another soldier, dropping to his knees to help the bleeding out man on the ground next to shaking a shaking Jones.

Jones' vision began to turn red, and little black lines began to sprawl across her view everywhere, almost like spider webs. She began to lose all feeling from her body, as well as control. She had almost not even noticed that she had her hands around the throat of another soldier and was squeezing hard, cracking her teammates' trachea. The soldier yelled before the crack, but Jones couldn't make out a single word he said. It was like it was nonsense. More nonsense came from behind Jones as she realized another soldier had driven a knife into her shoulder. She didn't even feel it. She quickly turned and bit into the neck of the woman, and tore away a mix of flesh and veins. Blood poured all over the front of Jones as she swallowed the hunk of flesh whole and went back for another bite. It was refreshing. The flesh tasted delicious and she craved more. Her vision was completely dark red now and the black lines clouded her line of sight. Her consciousness was becoming less and less by the second. She looked around and saw 2 more of her teammates laying, spasming among the worms as well. This didn't bother her. She turned back to her meal and took another bite, tearing away a chewy hunk of meat from the soldier's leg. Blood coated her chin and mouth but Jones didn't care. She was so hungry.

"Squad A, if you can hear me, we are pulling back! Main evacuation is complete and reinforcements have arrived!" Jones heard the words but they made no sense to her. Again, nonsense. She continued to feed.

Overhead, a loud chopping sound passed over and Jones looked up. Through the fading vision and consciousness Jones made out the view of several helicopters flying by. Jones could only think of one thing-more food. She stood up from her meal, which was now old, and raised her head to the sky. She had almost completely faded. She faced the direction of the helicopter's flight path and let out a long, high pitched screech that echoed off the city walls. She then took off on a dead sprint towards the new set of reinforcements in the distance. Her world then completely went black.

Private Jones was gone.

ELEVEN

Miller sat alone in the corner of his prison cell, staring at the wall. He couldn't believe the stupidity of the man in charge of this fort. He had experienced the loss of his world at the hands of nature, while this world would be lost at the hands of arrogance. The Colonel was an egomaniac who refused to do things any other way than his, even if it meant losing the lives of millions of people. He sure as hell had proven that during their little meeting in his office. The man would pay dearly someday for his mistakes, and Miller thought that, that day would be coming very soon.

He glanced around the rest of the room that contained other prison cells. To his right in the large cell were all 11 of the civilians that he had luckily managed to escort from their doomed dimension. They were 1 short from when they had entered the bridge, but considering what had happened, Miller was amazed that this was all that they had lost. In with them were his 2 remaining soldiers, the kid Edwards and Corporal Hudson. They had lost 4 men since coming through the bridge. 4 men that died so the rest of these innocents could live out the rest of their lives free of fear, but that was before they knew how fucked the situation in this dimension was becoming.

Miller looked over to his left and saw another cell with the 4 remaining soldiers from the lab facility. He wasn't sure what their names were, other than Staff

Sergeant Rodriguez. The man seemed like a brave soldier who cared deeply about doing his job. This was a man that Miller felt he could understand, because he was the same way; but while leaving the lab, he had seen part of Rodriguez die. When the man he had called, Pots died, so did a piece of Rodriguez's soul. The man spent the entire ride to the fort breaking down over the death. He had watched the last of his family die, a problem that Miller knew far too much about, and could share with him; the only issue was that Miller felt that Pots' death had been his fault. Miller had been the one to come through the bridge. He had linked the two dimensions. He had heard something about terrorists destroying the arc and causing this, but the way Miller looked at it, the problem wouldn't have happened if he had not requested access to the bridge. Now good men were dead, and this dimension was likely doomed, just like his.

Miller watched the 4 men from the lab, curiously. They seemed to work well as a team and cared for one another. Rodriguez sat alone in the corner of the cell, clearly thinking about past events, just like Miller was. Rodriguez then looked up and met Miller's eyes with his.

"How are you holding up, man?" asked Rodriguez. He seemed to be much calmer now as compared to the state of mind he was in leaving the facility.

"Shit man, as good as I can be when the world ends." Miller replied. He was being honest but trying to cover up how truly shitty he felt. After a few moments of silence Rodriguez spoke up.

"Sorry about your world. I know it must be tough dealing with that shit and then dealing with this. Actually, I wouldn't know. I can't begin to understand. All I can say is you and your people deserve better." The man was sincere. Miller could tell he was kind and caring, but he still felt guilty for what he had done.

"No need to be sorry. None of this is your fault. If anything, I am sorry for your friend Pots and your team. You two seemed close." Miller said. Rodriguez's expression saddened and he looked towards the floor.

"Pots was a great man. My best friend. He was like a brother to me. I still can't believe he is gone. He was all the family that I had left." Rodriguez said, his eyes swelling with tears. He quickly wiped them away and looked up smiling. "You stayed back and saved me. You tried to save him too. I appreciate that, man. Really, I do." Miller and Rodriguez gave small grins to one another in appreciation. The room stayed quiet for another moment.

"I met Pots before- well, you know." said Edwards from across the room. "He was a good man. He saved my life and some of these people too. We won't forget that, ever."

Rodriguez smiled at the kid, seeing that his brother had made a lasting impression.

"And now we are in this shit situation after all of that." said Alan, who sat on the bench staring off into space. "I don't know about all of you, but I am getting really sick of sitting in here being treated as a criminal for no reason." This was something they all agreed on.

"The only criminal here is that bastard, Hodge. Y'all work for him?" asked Miller.

"Unfortunately yes, but as you can see that doesn't matter anymore." replied a young kid from the corner of the cell, sitting on the floor playing with rocks.

"Shit Rookie, at least you only had to work with him for a couple weeks! It's going on a year for me, and who knows how long for Rodriguez! Old bastard." Walt said with a chuckle.

"Real funny, Walt." Rodriguez said with a sad smile. "I wish I never had to work for him. Corrupt fucker. I feel bad for all of you though. You are locked up because he doesn't even deem you as people. Thats fucked up."

Miller frowned and clenched his hand into a fist thinking about what the Colonel had told him before about shooting all of his people.

"He calls us 'The Others'." said Miller, with hate in his tone. "But apparently it's not just us he wants dead. Fucker refuses to even warn your own military about the bridge events and infected. He didn't believe me." This really got Rodriguez's attention.

"What are you talking about?" Rodriguez said, his tone changing to anger.

"It's starting. The bridge events the doctor spoke of. The National Guard are fighting against a bridge as we speak and Hodge refused to warn them" Miller said, clenching his fist harder. "He has your doctor working on something in handcuffs. I'm not sure what."

"That mother fucker. He's going to get countless people killed for his own ego." Rodriguez now looked more pissed than others. "Pots didn't die for this shit."

The room was silent. Nobody spoke as they pondered the news they had just received about their commander.

"There is good news, however. He mentioned that General McCalister heard about us and is coming to check up on the situation himself." Miller said to break the silence.

"This is good news. McCalister is a good man. If anyone can get us out of this shit its him." replied Walt.

"Shit, I'll just be happy to get off this floor. I'm running out of rocks to play with!" Rookie said as he flicked a rock against the far wall. The men all gave a chuckle.

Miller wanted to go further in his confessions with the men. It felt good to talk to people who respected him. He needed to get his guilt off his chest about the bridge, but before he could, the door to the prison chamber flew open. In through the door walked Major LeBlanc with two of the black armored soldiers at his side, which Miller had previously learned were Hodge's personal guards. He rounded the doorway and stepped into the open room, facing all of the prisoners.

"Miller, your presence has been requested by Colonel Hodge. He needs to speak to you in his office immediately." LeBlanc said, pulling out a pair of handcuffs.

"Fuck you, man. I am not going anywhere in those cuffs. I am done with them." Miller said. LeBlanc sighed.

"Look, I can either force them on you, or you can willingly wear them." LeBlanc said, the man to his left over eagerly pulling out a nightstick from his belt. Seeing this out of the corner of his eye, LeBlanc came close to the cell and spoke quietly. "Look marine, you don't want to do this in front of your people. Think of the kid." LeBlanc's voice was stern, but had a hint of sympathy. Miller looked over towards the large cell of civilians. The little girl from the group was against the bars, watching intensely. LeBlanc was right.

"Ah alright. But you gotta take me to dinner before you do this kinky handcuff shit." Miller said, trying to be a smartass. He would go willingly but he would keep running his mouth. What surprised him, however, was the slight smirk that crossed LeBlanc's face. Maybe this man wasn't half bad. He was just following orders after all.

Miller stepped out of his cell as the door opened. He put out his arms and willingly wore the cuffs. LeBlanc walked ahead of him with his two guards taking up the rear and the men all walked to Hodge's office together.

When Miller reached the office, Hodge was already behind his desk, waiting. Doctor Allen was still in the same chair that he was in when Miller had been dragged away before. At a quick glance it looked like Allen was working on mapping the bridge events and trying to predict future trends. Miller was curious but there was no time.

"Miller, sit." Hodge said, his face stern and angry.

"What is this all about?" Miller asked, annoyed that he had to be in this place again.

"Tell me more about these worms." Hodge said bluntly.

"They found them, didn't they? They found them, and their operation failed, didn't it." Miller said. It wasn't a question. He already knew the answer. The Colonel had played games and it had cost lives.

"It wasn't a complete failure. The main evacuation was a success, however the National Guard lost around 168 soldiers in the evacuation." Hodge said not batting an eye. He didn't seem at all bothered. "These deaths were necessary to further understand the enemy."

"Necessary? Are you fucking kidding me? This all could have been prevented if you just listened to the doctor and I earlier today! You played games and people died!" Miller exclaimed, his face red with anger. Hodge did not like this comment.

"You watch your tone, son. I didn't ask for your two cents on the situation. Reinforcements have arrived and are cleansing the city. Trapped civilians are being evacuated. I didn't ask for your opinions, I asked for your help!" yelled Hodge.

"So after people die you want my help? You are a twisted man. Who is to say you will even listen this time!" Miller yelled in the Colonel's face. The Colonel stood up and got into Miller's face, so close that when he yelled, spit hit Miller's cheeks.

"You've got a smart mouth, son! You have an attitude and authority issue. I will see to it that that is fixed! Right now, however, I need information and you will give it to me!" Hodge screamed.

Miller held his tongue. Arguments could wait. If Hodge actually listened, this was more important.

"What do you need to know?" asked Miller, gritting his teeth.

"Everything. What are they? How do they work?" asked Hodge, now sitting back down.

Miller took a deep breath preparing for the ridicule. He knew of course. He just was preparing for the Colonel to not believe him, more than he already did not.

"These worms. They aren't just worms. As I've told you before. They are aliens of some sort. The lab geeks back where I came from said they were some form of nematode, but I don't fully understand what that even means." Miller paused, expecting Hodge to roll his eyes, but this time he didn't. He continued. "All that I can tell you for certain is that they act as some sort of parasite, turning the host into a predator."

"What do you mean, a predator?" asked Hodge, interested.

"I mean they burrow into the host, and make them bloodthirsty. All they want to do is feed. They feed on fresh meat. Anything that moves is fair game, but for some reason they prefer people. I have never understood why." Miller said, thinking back to all his times facing the infected in combat. "Once in the host, after some time passes they begin to somehow mutate and make them more efficient killers. Size, claws, teeth, strength, you name it, they develop it; but this takes time and when newly infected, they are unrecognizable as monsters."

"The perfect infiltrator and hunters." Hodge said, a little too intrigued. Miller brushed off his annoyance and continued.

"When the parasite enters your system, it takes control of everything. We dissected the infected and it was mind blowing. Although these worms start only 3 inches long, once in the body they grow. They tap first into the nervous system just below the brain on the spine. That gives them control. The hosts don't feel pain, they don't get tired, they no longer can reason. At this point they are gone, basically dead. Then they begin to take over other systems like the digestive." Miller said.

"Why would they do that?" Hodge asked, now very interested.

"The parasites have no way to feed. They are basic organisms. In order to feed they must feed using another creature's digestive system, so they pirate it and feed on meat." Miller said with disgust. The Colonel seemed like he was enjoying this almost.

"The only weakness is to keep the nervous and digestive systems running, the host needs to be alive. Once the parasite is tapped into the host, they are connected. Kill the host you kill the parasite. There is no separating the two." Miller ended with. He glanced up at Hodge who had a sick expression on his face. "It would also be good to keep in mind that these worms may sometimes infect animals as well. It is rare, but I have seen it. I hope that nobody ever has to see the creations that come from that mess."

"This is very interesting, indeed. Thank you for that. The better we understand our enemy the better we can fight them." Hodge said; but Miller felt there was more to it.

"Sir, don't try to use these things for gain. You will fail. They are no bio-weapons." Miller said hesitantly. Hodge simply ignored him and moved on.

"The reason I need to know these things, Miller, is simple. After Syracuse, General McCalister placed me in charge of evacuation efforts in New York State. I am in control now." Hodge said with a smug tone.

"McCalister isn't coming?" Miller said, cautiously, worrying about the fate of his people now.

"No he is not. But I want to cut you a deal." said Hodge grinning arrogantly. "If you assist me in planning and provide your expertise, I will release your people."

Miller didn't like this. He hated the man even though he hardly knew him but had no other option; but he did have 1 request.

"You release Staff Sergeant Rodriguez and his team too. If you do that it's a deal." Miller said.

Hodge thought for a couple seconds, frowning at the offer but finally gave in.

"It goes against my better judgement but you have a deal. Just have it known that if you cross me, I will personally lock every one of those people up for the rest of their short lived lives." Hodge said, scowling at Miller. He was serious and Miller knew it. Now was his time to make a difference and stop what he started.

TWELVE

Gently pulling the blinds aside, Jessica peered anxiously out the hospital window to look at the view of the city. It was gone. The whole city was lost. The view of the city in the distance showed nothing but flames and smoke. The view closer to the hospital showed nothing but blood stained walls, mutilated bodies, walls pockmarked with bullet holes, and abandoned vehicles. The National Guard force that had come to evacuate this city had fought tooth and nail to get everyone they could out. For hours the sounds of gunshots, screams and explosions filled the city; but it was dusk now and the sounds of war had been silent for hours now. Every now and then Jessica would hear the sound of a helicopter passing overhead, or the sound of gunshots in the distance, but the main battle was lost now along with the city. The view of the destruction was horrifying, but not nearly as horrifying as what Jessica could see on the streets below.

It had been at least 2 hours now since the bridge downtown had closed itself, but it managed to unload so many of the terrifying beasts into the city that they now swarmed the streets in waves of thousands. She had checked the window every few minutes to see if the hiding spot in the hospital had been discovered yet, and she thanked the lord that it had not. She was luckier than most of the survivors who hadn't been evacuated. Every now and then she would hear screams as the beasts discovered survivor after survivor and dragged them out onto the street to be eaten alive. Although she was safe for now, she knew it was only a matter of time before they had gotten into here as well.

"God damn. That's not terrifying or anything." said Corporal Jackson, looking out the window just behind Jessica. Jessica had discovered the man and his squad mate, Private Thompson, while making a run to look for an evacuation site just 3 hours ago.

Jessica had made it to the hospital building with 2 other survivors remaining from her group. Barely escaping a swarm running out of an alley that had taken the others of her group, she had gotten a man named Tyrel and a woman named Sharron to safety. Tyrel was a large, strong man. His dark toned face was littered with small scars that he claimed he had received from an IED in Iraq years ago. He was a veteran, and it showed through his courage. Jessica wasn't sure she would have made it back to the hospital if it weren't for him. He had helped them through hell and pushed them forward. Although Tyrel was helpful, Sharron was the complete opposite. She was a skinny framed, blonde woman who seemed to care more about the condition of her suit jacket than those around her. She had spent the entire time hiding, whining and complaining about what was going on; almost like she hadn't realized everyone else was experiencing it too. Once the group had entered the building, they had discovered that the building was empty. Everyone had been evacuated. Everyone except 2 of the security guards who had been out looking for survivors when the National Guard came. They had been left behind. The upside was that they were both armed and that made Jessica feel a little safer.

The group had sat in the safety of the hospital throughout the battle that raged all around the city, hoping for help to come back. They prayed that the military would beat these things, or at least make another sweep through, but after an hour and half of waiting, Jessica realized it wasn't going to happen. She volunteered to make a run to search for an evacuation site to bring help back and the two security guards joined her. The street outside of the hospital thankfully had not been swarmed yet and it allowed the group a safe exit. Jessica had figured the smartest place to go would be to head towards the closest shooting. It was a risk, but a necessary one. As they snuck through the alleyways and crossroads, she saw 2 soldiers running full speed at them from the opposite direction. The men spotted the group and screamed to run. None of them understood why until a group of dozens of the beasts sprinted out of the alleyway, chasing the men. Jessica turned and ran with the soldiers as they passed by, but the two security guards stayed put, shocked by the sight. Jessica stopped and yelled at the men to come with them, and while one did, the other drew his pistol and fired at the oncoming creatures. He managed to fire off 4 shots from his glock before he was overtaken. Jessica and the others ran back to the hospital, managing to lose the group chasing them, which had been distracted by the fresh meat.

The group had successfully made it back to their somewhat safe hiding spot when the soldiers gave them good and bad news. The bad news was that their Platoon had been overrun while defending the evacuation and there was no safe way out now. The good news was that they had a radio. The soldiers had called for an Evac chopper, telling command that they had found lost survivors but no answer came. White noise. That was about the same time that the battle had stopped. The National Guard had been overrun, and there was no telling when help would come.

Jessica tried to think of a plan but came up with nothing. The hospital was surrounded and there was nothing that they could do. There was nowhere they could go.

"Command, come in, Command." said Thompson trying the radio again. The young man hadn't let up since the first call failed to be acknowledged. The young man was shaking from fear, and every word he spoke was spoken with a trembling voice. "Command. Please. Anyone."

"Fuck those pricks. We are just grunts to them. What do they care if we live or die!" yelled Jackson as he kicked over a wheeled cart. The clash of metal sounded all through the hospital.

"Hey! You need to calm down right now. Are you trying to get us killed?" asked Tyrel, quietly. The man had remained calm this entire time amazingly. Jackson stopped his yelling and turned to face Tyrel, having to look up at the massive man.

"Well we might as well already be dead at this point! Nobody is coming! We are fucked!" snapped Jackson with a snarky tone, as he walked past Tyrel, shoving him with his shoulder as he passed. The man was trying to start a fight but Tyrel just rolled his eyes and shook his head.

"They can't just leave us! I am an American citizen! My attorney will hear about this!" cried Sharron, tears streaming down her face as she held her cell phone close to her chest and further sobbed. "And now my phone is dead!"

"Sharron, I don't want to be the bearer of bad news, but I don't think there is anything your attorney can do about this." Tyrel said, with a slight smirk on his face. The woman was a mess and used to being pampered. The apocalypse is what she needed to put her in her place.

"Oh quit your fucking crying you dumb bitch!" snapped Jackson as he turned and walked over to Sharron.

"Hey man, there's no need for that." said Juan, the security guard. He took a step forward to watch the disrespectful soldier.

"*There's no need for that.*" Jackson said, mocking Juan's accent. "Fuck you man! Fuck you and fuck this whole city!" He now got into Juan's face and continued to yell. "I didn't join the army to sit here and get told what I can and can't do by some Mexican!" He jabbed Juan in the chest with his finger and spat at his shoes. "I am in charge!"

"The hell you are! And I'm an American, just like you!" Juan said, shoving Jackson's hand away.

"Oh that's gold. You're an American and I'm the fucking president." Jackson said with an arrogant chuckle.

"Don't bring that racist shit in here! We could have easily left you in the street!" yelled Tyrel, still minding his noise. "Shut your shit down, and take a seat." He said calmly yet sternly.

Jackson still stared into Juan's face, ready to start a fight still.

"Y'all didn't save me. I saved y'all and I'm not gonna take shit from this illegal." Jackson said, hatefully. The man was the personification of all the issues going on within the nation, aside from the bridge of course.

"You're no better than those cultists out west." said Jessica finally. The comment took everyone aback, finally hearing the quiet woman add her thoughts.

"Yeah well maybe they got the right idea." Jackson said. He turned to Jessica this time. "With that said, I'm not taking no shit from some little bitch either. You need to learn some fucking manners!" Jackson said as he stepped towards Jessica, raising his hand to strike her. Before he could however, Jackson was struck in the face and dropped to the floor. Above him stood Juan, rubbing his fist.

"Someone needs to teach *you* some fucking manners, white boy." Juan said, with a satisfied grin on his face. Everyone else's faces showed slight grins as well, except for Thompson who sat in the corner still working at the radio.

"You-you broke my fucking nose!" Jackson said, holding his face. Blood streamed down from his chin. He spat blood on the ground and Jessica noticed a little white object in it. "And you knocked out a tooth!" Jackson yelled in anger. Before he could retaliate, Juan knocked him back to his stomach and placed a pair of handcuffs on the man.

"Until help comes, you stay in these. We can't trust you." Juan said, still grinning.

"Now that's a great idea." said Tyrel in agreement.

"Fuck you! Fuck you all! We are all dead anyway! You'll see!" Jackson yelled, blood still covering and dripping from his face.

"Let's stick him in that room down the hall for now." Jessica said, leading Juan and his prisoner from the desk to a hospital room.

"You can't do thi-" Jackson yelled as he was cut off by the door shutting in his face.

"There. Now let's figure things out quietly." Tyrel said, letting out a slow, deep breath.

"Somebody come in. We are locked inside the Community Hospital with civilians. We need evac." said Thompson into the radio again, his voice still shaky.

Jessica peered out of the window again. Off in the distance she heard gunfire, but it was nowhere near them.

The military must have had the city surrounded. Help was out there.

"Should I make another run for help?" asked Jessica. Everyone around her seemed amazed by her bravery.

"Jessica, last time we went out, the street was empty. It's swarmed now. You'll never make it." Juan said, sounding impressed by her offer.

"Yes, but there is no other way. Help isn't coming. They will find us eventually. We need to do something." Jessica said. "It's the only way."

The group sat in silence, with the exception of the muffled yells of Jackson in the other room and Sharron sobbing against the wall.

"Alright. I don't like it, but she's right. There is no other way." Tyrel said.

"Okay then. I will head out and-" Jess said, being stopped by Tyrel who held a hand up.

"You already went once, Jessica. And we all thank you for that; but you aren't going to go again." Tyrel said.

"Well I'm not going out there! I'm a somebody! I'm too important to die!" cried Sharron. Tyrel rolled his eyes.

"Nobody is being forced out there, Sharron. Relax. I will go." Tyrel said in his deep, calm voice.

"No. It was my idea. I will go. Nobody is dying for me." Jessica said defiantly. Tyrel grinned at her stubbornness.

"Nobody is dying. Anyway, I am faster than you. I was in the military years ago, and once a soldier, always a soldier. Let me do this." he said calmly while smiling.

"Well you can't go alone. I'm going too." Jessica said.

"That's right. He can't go alone. So I am going." said Juan. "Besides. I am the one with a gun." He motioned to the pistol on his hip.

"Great. Then that's all we need. Jessica stays here. We go get help and that's final." Tyrel said smiling at Jessica. She didn't like being told what to do, especially when it was by someone who thought she couldn't do it, but this wasn't the case. They were right. Tyrel was faster, and Juan did have a gun. Protection was his job after all. She sighed and looked up.

"Fine. But if you don't make it back, I am going and there is no stopping me." she said. Tyrel smiled at her.

"Deal. But if we are going, we need to go now before they find us." he said.

Before anyone could agree, Thompson spoke up from the corner.

"Actually, it looks like you may not have to." he said. His voice finally sounded calmed. He had good news.

"Squad A of Platoon Charlie, National Guard to command, over." Thompson said into the radio. The room fell completely silent while waiting for a response. Finally after a few seconds of anticipation, a response came through.

"Good to hear from you, son! We knew more of you had to be out there somewhere! What's your sit-rep, over?" a happy voice with a southern accent said from the other end. The group all cheered and looked back to Thompson. There was still hope yet.

"Sir, there are 2 of us left from our Platoon. Everyone else is gone. We are held up in Community Hospital in the city with 4 civilians. We are surrounded and need immediate evacuation." Thompson said, rocking back and forth eagerly.

"God damn, son. You have done a fine job out there and it is your lucky day! I happen to have a black hawk at my disposal that will arrive at your location in 10 minutes for pick up!" said the voice on the other end. The group, all filled with joy, began to hug one another. Tears of happiness ran down Jessica's face.

"Thank you, sir. We will be on the roof, marking our location with red flares." Thompson said, all fear gone from his voice this time.

"Godspeed, soldier." the voice said before the channel went dead.

"Thank god! I can get out of this awful place!" cried Sharron.

"Looks like nobody needs to go out there now." said Juan. "Should we break the news to that asshole, Jackson?" Nobody answered. As if all realizing how silent the room was at the same time, they all stood up. There hadn't been any yells or sounds of struggle for several minutes now.

"Jackson? Hey Jax, you there, bro?" said Thompson. There was no response. Thompson grabbed his rifle that was propped against the reception desk.

"Maybe he passed out?" Juan suggested.

"No way. He was too full of energy. Anyway, you only slugged him once." Tyrel said, creeping towards the door to the hospital room.

"Jax man. You gotta answer me, brother." Thompson said, now holding the door handle. There was no answer, and in the silence they heard the slam of something on metal. Thompson opened the door. "What the fuck!" he cried, raising his rifle to the ceiling.

Across the floor from where Jackson was laying, was a pool of blood that had a trail leading away from it smeared across the floor. The blood smear then continued up the wall and led to the open ceiling vent where Jackson's shredded legs were hanging out. The body slammed into the vent again and again as something inside was trying to pull it further in.

"Oh my god." Thompson said, choking on his own words. He was too shocked to do anything.

"Shoot it, man!" yelled Tyrel at the young soldier who suddenly snapped back to attention.

Thompson raised his rifle, clicking the fire switch to full auto, and blasted the ceiling, swaying his gun back and forth, unleashing the 30 round magazine within seconds. He yelled until the gun clicked, empty. The man stood in place, still holding the rifle toward the ceiling as smoke rolled off the barrel. He panted and listened for noise. Silence. Dark blood trickled from the bullet holes that punched through the vent and speckled the ground below, making little dripping noises. The shredded legs of Corporal Jackson slid back slightly from the vent entrance.

"I think I got it." said Thompson quietly.

"I certainly hope so." said Tyrel, looking at the spent magazine Thompson had so liberally fired into the ceiling.

"How did it find him? It's almost like it knew he was there!" cried Sharron. This was the smartest comment that the woman had made in hours. The group sat in silence for a few moments while thinking. Jessica remembered the blood soaked face of Jackson as they threw him into the room. That had to be it.

"Can they smell blood? He was bleeding. That is the only thing that makes sense, right?" Jessica said, hesitantly. The rest of the group pondered it and agreed.

"Shit, this gets worse and worse. There's blood everywhere now! We have to move!" Juan said, looking around the room for anything else that seemed off.

"The chopper is on its way. He is right. But we can't just leave Jackson up there like that." said Thompson looking back to the shredded mess that was his fellow soldier. "He was an asshole, but he was still my teammate."

"I will help you." said Juan, most likely feeling a little guilty for putting him in the room. "But let's make it quick."

The two men stepped up onto a pair of chairs and eased the bloody pulp of a body down from the vent and onto the floor. The dripping pile of meat made a wet slap as it landed on the tile floor. The beast had made quick work of the man. Skull showed on half his head from where flesh had been stripped off. His upper body was torn open so wide that half of his remaining organs were hanging out like gory piñatas. His legs were the best looking part of him and even those looked like raw hamburger. The man had suffered a fate worse than death. He had been eaten alive.

"There. He is down. There is nothing else we can do for him. We need to leave now." Tyrel said, eager to leave this place.

"They got him up there so easily." Juan said, amazed at the strength of the beasts.

As the group stood around, preparing to make the trip to the roof, a muffled noise came from the ceiling.

"Oh no. There are more." said Thompson to himself as he dropped his spent magazine and slammed another into the rifle. Juan also pulled his pistol and looked up to the ceiling.

Still standing beneath the vent, Juan looked up into the darkness as a small, grey object fell from the hole and landed onto his face.

"God damn! What the hell is this?" Juan yelled as he frantically grabbed at his left eye.

"Let me see!" ordered Thompson as he spun Juan around to examine the eye he was holding. Jessica also rushed over to lend her assistance.

She looked and saw the tail end of what looked like a worm disappear into the corner of Juan's eye. The bulge from the creature wiggled under the skin of his eyelid and disappeared behind the eyeball. Blood streamed from the corner of his eye socket as he cried in agony.

"It's in my eye! Get it out! Get it out!" he screamed in pain, whipping his head back and forth in his hands.

"I can't see it! I don't know where it went!" yelled Jessica as she held a flashlight into the struggling man's face.

"Ah! My fucking head! It hurts! It hurts so much!" he cried as he dropped to his knees and began shaking uncontrollably.

"What's going on with him?" asked Thompson, the shaking now returning to his voice.

"I don't know! Hold him still!" Jessica yelled. Thompson grabbed Juan and held him as tightly as he could, but the man shook free. He began to scream as he struggled with Thompson and his scream began to sound high pitched and animal-like.

"What the fuck was that?" yelled Thompson as he held onto Juan again.

Suddenly Juan stopped screaming and stopped shaking. Thompson still held him as Juan looked into Thompson's eyes. Juan's eyes which were once brown and clear, were now bloodshot and black. His stare was dead and he looked deeply at Thompson. He licked his lips and bloody drool ran down Juan's salt and pepper beard.

"Juan, bro. Are you good?" Thompson asked. "Why the hell are you looking at me like that?" he said. What happened next answered his question.

Juan bent his head back, opened his mouth as wide as he could manage, and snapped his head forward, biting deeply into the side of Thompson's neck. As Thompson screamed in surprise and pain, Juan snapped his head to the side and tore away a hunk of meat, splattering the white walls around the two men with fresh blood. Juan slurped up the cords of flesh and gulped as he swallowed the chunk whole. Fresh blood ran down the side of Juan's mouth and dribbled off of his chin as he went back for another bite. Before he could clamp down again, Jessica had grabbed a chair and smashed it over the back of Juan's head, knocking the crazed man to the floor. Without feeling the pain of the hit, Juan shot back up and dived at Jessica. He knocked her to the ground and climbed on top of her. She felt his hot breath on her face and just before he could bite into her, a gunshot sounded and blood splattered the wall above Jessica as Juan's brains blew out of his forehead. She quickly shoved the body off of her and saw Thompson, barely alive with blood squirting from his neck, holding Juan's pistol in his shaky hands. Jessica looked down at the empty holster at Juan's hip and sighed in relief. She quickly stood up and ran to Thompson, although there was nothing she could do.

"Get-get." Thompson wheezed words out as he fell to his back in the pool of his own blood. "Get to the roof." He was pale and was losing his blood fast. "Here." he said as he handed Jessica a flare. "Go." He said before going limp on the ground.

"Shit. We have to go now! More are coming!" yelled Tyrel, looking out of the window. He ran over to Jessica and helped her to her feet. "Sharron! Let's go!"

The group ran out to the hall and ran towards the stairway. Behind them they heard the clatter of creatures filling the area that they had just left. They were fast and hungry.

"Go! Get to the roof!" yelled Jessica as she slammed the stairway door shut behind her.

The trio ran up the stairs as fast as they could to reach the roof. Just 4 more floors. It wasn't far, but the distance wasn't the issue. The issue was the gaining beasts.

They were now one more floor up, just 3 to go. Jessica and Tyrel were going as fast as they could but Sharron began to slow.

"Guys. Slow down! I can't keep up! I need to rest!" she cried as she slowed to a light jog.

"Move, Sharron! They are coming!" yelled Jessica, not stopping for the pampered woman.

"I can't go this fast! Help me!" yelled Sharon who now stood, panting in front of the door to the last floor Jessica and Tyrel had been on.

Just as Jessica turned to shout at Sharron, the door behind the woman cracked open and a pair of grey skinned, clawed hands grabbed the woman by her ankle.

"Help me! Don't leave me!" she cried at the other two. There was nothing they could do for her. The woman's scream became desperate as she was forced into the doorway that was still mostly closed. As the beast dragged her into the hallway from the stairway, her other leg caught the door, but this didn't stop the beast from pulling. She screamed in agony as her leg snapped loose from its socket and bent upwards toward her head. The door wasn't open enough to fit the woman and her limbs began to dislocate. With a final snap, her knee layed restless next to her head as she was dragged away into the hall.

"They are right on our asses! Move!" yelled Tyrel. His soldier instincts were kicking back in and adrenaline kept him moving.

1 more floor to go. Jessica was panting but pushed through her fatigue as she heard the screams of the creatures just a floor below. She moved as fast as she could. The exit to the roof was in sight, just ahead now. Pushing as hard as she could now, her legs burning from exhaustion, she burst through the doorway just behind Tyrel.

"There it is! I see the chopper!" yelled Tyrel. "Light the flare!"

Jessica pulled the flare from her pocket. It had blood smeared on it still from Thompsons wound but it would still light. Quickly she struck it several times and red smoke burst from the end of it as it ignited. She tossed it to the ground.

"Just a minute out." she said, looking off at the black vehicle coming towards them. The sound of the chopping from the rotors was becoming clearer. She was so distracted by the sight that she forgot momentarily about the creatures running after them. She hadn't closed the door.

"Jessica! Watch out!" yelled Tyrel as a beast burst through the doorway and slammed Jessica up against the concrete wall to the side of the door. Her head smacked the hard surface and she blinked away the red blurred vision and stars. Expecting to see one of the grey creatures, she was surprised to see a crazed, female, soldier. Her short, brown hair was coated with dried blood, the same with around her mouth. Tiny, red strands of meat were stuck between her teeth. Her army fatigues were torn and stained as well. The tag on her uniform read, Jones. She was one of the National Guard soldiers. Her bloodshot, dark eyes focused on Jessica's neck as she felt her heart beat faster. She blinked away more stars and tried to yell for help, but the woman's hand around her throat made it impossible. The woman tried to bite Jessica's neck, but she pushed back as hard as she could. She heard the teeth snap together like an animal. She didn't want to die like this. She couldn't die like this. She pushed back harder now, forcing the woman to stumble backwards. Before the woman could do any more to Jessica, a pair of massive hands grabbed the crazed woman and threw her off of the rooftop. Jessica fell to the ground and looked up at the large frame of Tyrel, holding his hand out to help her up.

"Jessica, get up! The chopper is almost here!" Tyrel yelled. "Don't die on me now!"

Jessica got back to her feet and stumbled over to the edge of the building. The helicopter was almost there. She felt the wind of the blades spinning above her as it slowly lowered. Just then several more creatures burst through the doorway and sprinted at Jessica. This was it. There was no stopping this many.

"Get out of here! Save yourself!" yelled Tyrel as he ran at the creatures, wrapped them up in his large, muscular arms, and tackled them. They struggled against the massive man, and he grunted as he tried to keep his footing. One of the beasts bit into his bicep and tore away a ribbon of flesh. Another clawed at his thigh, trying to get free. There was no way that Tyrel could hold them much longer. Knowing that, he locked eyes with Jessica, looked back at his opponents, and threw himself off of the building still holding them, landing into the swarm many floors below.

"No!" Jessica yelled as she watched the only survivor left tumble away off of the side of the building.

More creatures flooded out of the doorway onto the roof now, but they were quickly cut down. The helicopter hovered next to the building ledge as its crew chief fired the M240 mounted machine gun into the oncoming beasts. They weren't going to get her today. A soldier hopped out of the troop bay of the helicopter and grabbed Jessica by the arm.

"Where are the others, miss? We need to get out of here now! There is a horde coming at this position!" yelled the soldier as he raised his rifle and fired a pair of shots into a creature climbing over the edge of the building it had just scaled. Jessica, babbling nonsense, finally got the words out she was trying to say.

"They are all dead. It's just me now." she said, in disbelief.

"Alright. Load up and let's get the hell out of here!" yelled the soldier as he pulled her and led her to the chopper. She climbed inside and looked out of the open door as the helicopter flew away. A couple of creatures ran from the building and jumped at the helicopter as it pulled away. One missed, tumbling to its death below while another managed to get its hands onto the edge of the troop bay. Before it could pull itself up, the crew chief drew his pistol and shot the creature in the head with a loud pop. It let go and fell to the ground below. Jessica was safe. She was alive and escaped. But there were many more who weren't so lucky. She thought of all of the people she had seen die in the past 24 hours and her stomach turned. Leaning out the doorway, she vomited.

"Are you okay, maam?" asked the soldier next to her, his face looking concerned. She didn't answer. She peered out at the view of the city from above. All over she saw the remnants of the city she used to work in. It was gone. Everywhere she looked she saw destruction and creatures.

"Wanna see something cool? Look out ahead." said the soldier, pointing. As Jessica followed his finger she saw the oncoming shape of a jet. It zoomed over the city, dropping bombs onto the crowds of beasts below it. They ignited into flames. She looked around and saw many other helicopters flying away from the city as well.

"Are those more survivors?" she asked hopefully.

"Yes ma'am. We tried to get everyone out that we could before starting the bombing. You are a lucky woman." said the soldier before turning away to talk into his radio.

Jessica looked below as they passed over the outskirts of the city and saw the full might of the United States military. Tanks and troops were everywhere below, engaging the oncoming hordes of beasts that made it past the bombing. She sat back in her seat and breathed deeply. She was out. She survived.

"Make me proud." said the words of her husband in her head. She would. She would do all she could to make him proud. She had fought hard to make it out alive and did everything she could to save others, but it just didn't work out as planned. Next time she would be more prepared. Next time she would make a difference.

THIRTEEN

John was back at the facility that they had narrowly escaped with their lives. He couldn't believe that he was back there again and couldn't figure out why he was there either. He sat up and looked around. All that he saw was the tall, thick trees towering above him, casting their dark shadows on the tall grass in which he lay. There was an eerie feeling to the scenery, and the setting sun behind the distant hills wasn't helping. Just when he was starting to clear his head of his confusion, he heard a voice.

"Hey John! What you doin' down there on the ground? Don't you know there's work to be done!" said a deep voice of a large man whom he had known for years. Pots.

John stood up on his feet quickly and whipped his head around to see his burly friend. It was Pots. He was alive and here right in front of him!

"P-Pots?" John stuttered in disbelief. "Is it really you?"

"Of course it's me. What the hell are you talking about?" Pots replied, laughing. The sound of John's best friend's laugh filled him with joy. He smiled and began to walk forward.

He was relieved. The mission, the bridge, the monsters, all of it. It was all just a bad dream and Pots was alive. He was here in front of him. John began to walk faster now, ready to embrace his long lost brother in a

*well needed hug when he heard the unmistakable scream
of an infected beast. He froze. He turned towards the trees
and saw the tall, toned, grey body of a creature sprinting
through the shrubs towards Pots. Its veins bulged, and
bloody drool streamed through the air behind it as it ran.*

"Pots! Run!" yelled John at his friend.

*"What? I can't hear you!" Pots yelled back,
confused.*

*"Run! Look to your left!" yelled John again,
panicking. Pots was still confused and not turning around.
John tried to run but his feet felt like bricks weighing him
down. He tried to yell but Pots seemed to get further and
further away.*

*"Pots!" screamed John as he watched the beast
dive onto his friend and tear him into ribbons of flesh,
staining the green grass with red.*

The past wasn't a dream. This was, and John was
reliving what he was trying to repress.

*John tried to look away from the gruesome scene
he had already experienced once before, but couldn't. His
view focused on the gore and John began to sob. Then his
view went black as the sun set behind the hill and the trees.
He breathed heavily now and listened to the sound of
grass rustling and twigs breaking near him as something
approached. He tried to lift his arms but was paralyzed.
The sound of his own breathing was drowned out by a
gurgling and in front of him Pots appeared. His face was*

inches from John's, blood pooled in his mouth as he choked on it. Fear was in his friend's eyes as tears ran down his face. Pots spoke.

"End this shit." These were Pots' last words. John remembered this. He had been told by his friend to end what they were there for the start of.

"Pots-" John whimpered out before he was cut off by his own gasp. Suddenly in front of his face, Pots' face turned grey. His eyes bulged from his skull and turned bright red with his dark pupils dilated. Needle teeth lined his mouth and he ran a dark tongue across his now cut up and blood stained lips.

"P-Pots?" John whimpered again, pleading. Pots suddenly screamed and bit down on John's face.

John awoke screaming.

"Jesus Christ, Rodriguez. You okay, man?" said a concerned Rookie who shot up from his seated position at the foot of his bunk. Next to him sat Edwards, who also looked concerned. The young soldier had taken a liking to John's squad and was spending time with them. Edwards had briefly gotten to know Pots back at the facility and too shared the guilt of the man's death.

"I-I'm fine. I'm fine." John panted. "Just a bad dream." He was drenched with sweat and sat up from his bunk and looked around the barracks. Soldiers were all around staring but quickly got back to their own business.

"You sure, sir?" asked Edwards who looked like he already knew what the issue was.

"I'm fine, guys, really." John replied as he wiped the beads of sweat from his forehead. He desperately wanted to discuss the dream but these two kids weren't the people he needed.

"Anyone seen Miller?" asked John, trying to change the subject. "I still need to thank him for getting us out of those cells and into these beds."

"Lieutenant Miller has been spending a lot of time with Colonel Hodge in the command center. He has been assisting him with statewide evacuation plans, but everyone needs a break now and then. Maybe he's outside somewhere." said Edwards.

"I know Walt and Alan are outside trying to get news on the other bridge events. Maybe he is with them?" Rookie suggested.

"All right then. Let's get out of here. I'm sick of napping anyway." John replied, standing up and grabbing his bag. Together, the 3 men left the barracks and walked out into the bright sunlight of the quad. Across the base at the tarmac, a black hawk helicopter had landed. John watched as several of Hodge's personal guards jogged away from the chopper lugging a large, sealed contaminate box, tailed by a couple scientists wearing hazmat suits.

"What do you suppose that is all about?" asked Rookie, curiously. John had a couple ideas of what twisted things Hodge could be up to, but he pushed the thoughts aside.

"I don't know. Let's just keep moving." John replied.

The trio continued walking across the quad towards the offices, where sure enough, Walt and Alan were standing talking to Major LeBlanc. The trio continued to join the discussion.

"-so we have lost Syracuse, Albany, and various smaller cities so far. New York City is under siege currently. That's all the news that I can disclose for now, gentlemen." said Major LeBlanc to the two soldiers. He turned to see the approaching men and continued. "Ah, Sergeant Rodriguez! I see you are up!"

John, tailed by Rookie and Edwards, reached the group of men and halted. John let up a weak salute and replied, "Major."

"It's good to see that you are recovering well." LeBlanc replied. The smile faded off of his face when he saw that John wasn't smiling.

"No thanks to being locked in a cell, sir." John replied bitterly. John expected to be chewed out by his superior for his comment but to his dismay, the lecture didn't come. Just a moment of silence followed by a long sigh by LeBlanc.

"Gentlemen, would you please give the Sergeant and I a moment?" LeBlanc said to the 4 other men. They all quickly scuffled off towards the armory, no doubt to check their gear. After hearing nothing but news of failed missions, the men were all eager to be deployed and do some good. Unfortunately the order for deployment never came, but the men still prepared.

"Sergeant, I understand how you may feel about me and I will admit that I do not blame you." LeBlanc said calmly. John was caught off guard by the comment.

"What-" John said under his breath but LeBlanc continued.

"What I am about to say breaks the chain of command but it needs to be said. The way you were treated was wrong and if you want to blame me I understand. Nobody could expect what happened at Facility 12 and it wasn't your fault. I know that you lost a lot of good men up there including your friend Pots and I am sorry. It was wrong how Hodge treated you and your men and I hope you can forgive me for being involved."

John was taken aback. He had not expected this discussion from the officer.

"Sir, this means a lot to me and I need you to know that I don't blame you. I apologize for my comment, sir. I'm just dealing with a lot at the moment." John said, softly.

"And that's okay, John." LeBlanc said, now losing the formalities. "And I wish I could tell you it's all going to get better but that just isn't the case."

"Sir?" John asked, confused. LeBlanc sighed.

"Hodge has lost it. These events are popping up more frequently now, all over the east coast and through Canada now. These things are spreading and we are losing the fight. Doctor Allen is saying that there are now attacks around the world, but our east coast is seeing triple the bridge events.”

“Holy shit.” John replied in awe.

“As you know, Hodge has been tasked with leading the evacuation and defense of the state of New York as the military is spread thin. Well he is losing the fight and if you thought he was insane before, he is only getting worse. He is bitter, crazy, and playing with people's lives. This is becoming one big experiment for him.” LeBlanc said shaking his head in his hands.

“Where the hell is the General for all of this?” John asked.

“As I said. Leadership is spread thin. Last I heard, the General was held up in some old cold war bunker trying to command the defense of the further inland states. We are helpless and left to Hodge’s wrath.” LeBlanc said, glancing around. “Just thank god that we have Miller up in his command center trying to make some sane decisions.”

John thought back on the brave soldier who had run out of the first bridge just days ago. He had lost his whole world and was trying to save this one.

“I don't think I need to tell you that this discussion never happened, John.” LeBlanc said sternly.

“Secret is safe with me, sir.” John replied.

“Good. I just need you to prepare for the worst. Right now you, your men along with Miller and his are the most experienced personnel on this base; and when a bridge opens here, I want to be ready.” LeBlanc said.

"God forbid that happens." John replied. The Major paused for a second and spoke.

"The trends are showing more and more bridges opening all over the state, John. It's bound to happen and when it does, we need real leaders to save us all. I have served under Hodge, loyally, for 15 years and I have never seen the man like this before. He can't be trusted." LeBlanc said, shaking his head.

"I will do what I can, sir." John replied. The Major nodded and then walked away, back to the command center. John spoke to himself now remembering Pots' words. "I'm going to end this shit."

—

Miller sat in the command center with Hodge, Allen, and LeBlanc who had just entered the room.

"Major! Where the fuck have you been!" Hodge yelled at the man as he walked in.

"I was just getting some air, sir." LeBlanc said, stopping to salute.

"Breathe on your own fucking time, Major! You're on my time and we have a war to fight!" Hodge yelled, slamming his fist on the table. LeBlanc looked down at his feet and walked to the table to take a seat. Hodge now turned his anger to Allen. "Doctor! Give me a goddamn update on our situation. And use layman terms. I don't need my time wasted with this science shit."

The man was becoming more and more infuriating to be around. Something that just a couple days ago, Miller thought couldn't get worse but he was wrong. Loss after loss had begun to drive the man insane.

"Well sir, the bridge events are increasing at a rate that soon, we won't be able to defend against. Reports are showing bridges opening more frequently now as far out as the west coast, though still not at the rate the east coast is showing. Eastern Canada is being hammered by them as well and we have multiple reports from Europe and Asia now as well." Allen said with a shaky voice.

"And I don't suppose you have a solution thought up yet?" asked Hodge, irritated. Allen stayed silent. "You fuck up of a scientist. You have doomed us all."

Comments like this happened every couple hours. It was almost expected now, and Allen was still taking it to heart. The man turned away with tears in his eyes. Although these comments infuriated Miller, he was determined that it made these meetings smoother if he just kept his mouth shut.

"Major! What's the situation in New York?" Hodge said, now turning his attention to the officer. LeBlanc looked down at his laptop and spoke.

"Sir, I am seeing that the defense of the city fell hours ago, and there are still refugees trying to get out. In fact I am seeing now that a small section of the city on the Hudson is still making a stand while civilians await Evac." The Major said.

"And where is this Evac? Who hasn't authorized it yet?" Hodge asked, annoyed.

"Sir, they are waiting for you. You gave the order to hold all operations till you give the green light." Hodge said, monotone. His disrespect for his CO was starting to show.

"Don't tell me what I did, god dammit. I know my own orders, son!" yelled Hodge, trying to cover up his error. "What are we looking at down there?"

"Sir, the infected are closed in around the area really tight. A thin line of marines is all that is keeping them back for now. There are about 120 civilians at the docks waiting for Evac." LeBlanc said.

"God dammit, just send in some boats!" Hodge yelled. Miller finally spoke up.

"Sir, with that many people in that tight of a situation, choppers would be the better method." Hodge turned and glared at Miller.

"We don't have time to get choppers to that area." Hodge replied.

"Sir, any ship that you send to pick them up would have multiple birds on it." Miller replied, dumbfounded by the man's stupidity.

"Don't question my orders goddammit! If I say boats, we send boats!" Hodge yelled, red in the face.

"May I remind you that I have seen this before, and that I can tell you there may be things worse than infected humans out there. We don't have the time or resources to mount a boat operation." Miller said standing up.

"Sit your ass back down, Lieutenant! My orders are final!" Hodge yelled. Miller sat back down.

"We have another issue, sir." LeBlanc said, interrupting the argument. "Among the civilians are several United States senators who need immediate evacuation. Are we sure that this is the right course of action for such an important mission?"

Hodge walked silently over to Miller and LeBlanc. Leaning down in between the two of them he said in their ears, "Well then I hope they don't mind getting sea sick."

FOURTEEN

"Fire them up!" yelled the deck officer as Navy SEAL Petty Officer Jane Brummer hopped into the RHIB with her team. They were in the launch bay of the wasp class vessel, USS Iwo Jima, preparing for the evacuation mission into the Hudson River to rescue civilians trapped in New York City. Reports had been coming in non-stop of state of emergencies in all major cities in the northeastern United States. Reports of these mysterious portals opening up and releasing hell upon the people residing there were frequent. Brummer's team had been working around the clock non-stop on inland missions, trying to rescue high value targets and here they were again doing the same thing. Brummer, nor her team, had slept for nearly 27 hours now and were running on fumes. Around Brummer in the small boat were the 3 other soldiers in her fire team, with the other 4 members of her squad next to them in another boat. She sat up straight, preparing her mission briefing, and spoke as loud as she could; though she was exhausted and ready to pass out at any moment.

"Listen up team! I know we are all running on little to no sleep and are tired, but we just have this one mission left to run and I'm told we are promised a little bit of shut eye, so let's do this right!" The team all seemed to perk up at the mention of the opportunity for a little bit of rest after the mission. "Our mission here is simple! While the jar heads inside lower Manhattan hold back the assaulting wave of those creatures, we are to assist the navy in the transport of the remaining civilians back to the Iwo Jima for Evac! This includes 3 United States senators who were trapped within the city when it fell! We are to do this quickly, and we are to do this quietly! We all know from the past 3 days, that sound seems to attract these things, so be smart out there!"

"Ma'am, what are we getting for support on this mission? That's a big mission for two RHIBs to carry out." asked Seaman DeSanta. He of course was correct.

"We all know that the military is spread really thin right now, but the Colonel in charge of this mission, in all his wisdom, has granted us the use of two Navy SOC-R boats for support." replied Brummer.

"Well that's really helpful. How the hell are we going to evacuate that many people on 4 tiny boats? This will take forever!" replied DeSanta; and he was completely right. The RHIBs alone were tiny, and the special operations crafts they were assigned for support were useful for firepower, not personal capacity.

"I know, I know! But we have all been let down by brass before. We will just have to make as many trips as we can, and fast! Clear?" asked Brummer. The General consensus of the situation said 'this is fucked', but nobody complained aloud. "Alright people! These citizens aren't going to save themselves! Let's move out!"

The ship bay of the wasp vessel erupted with the sounds of charging firearms, yelling and boat engines firing up. All at once the vessels sped out of the bay and out onto the Hudson River. The two RHIBs led the charge with the SOC-Rs taking up the rear, guns at the ready. The marines behind the machine guns on the boats were tense, keeping their heads on a swivel. The spotlights from the boats tore through the dense darkness over the open water as the boats flew forward. The only light was from the ship, the full moon, and the flickers of fire in the distance.

"This mission is fubar." said DeSanta quietly to himself as he scanned the banks to their left through his night vision goggles. He had been grouchy the past two days, but then again, so would anyone who had seen the shit he had seen with as little sleep as he had. Brummer looked ahead at the man and noticed how stressed he was. He was breathing heavily, his M4 was shaking in his hands as he scanned the area around him. The man was ready to crash.

"Just keep up the good work, DeSanta, and you'll be home to your porno mags in no time! Shit, this is probably the longest you've ever gone without them!" replied Brummer, trying to improve the team's mood a bit. This got a few chuckles from the rest of the team, which was a good sign.

"Ah screw you. You know I hide those things too well for you to even know about them!" replied DeSanta, which got more chuckles from the team.

"Hey, I just thought it was safe to assume your lonely ass would need them." replied Brummer. After a few more minutes of the jabs back and forth to one another the conversation ended and everyone went serious again.

As the boat formation got further and further in on the river, the creepier things became. To the sides on the shoreline, flames flickered from past battles, illuminating destroyed buildings and blood stained ground in the darkness. The air smelled of rotting corpses and smoke while off in the distance were flashes followed by the distant sounds of gunshots from the final stand the marines were making in the city. One of the boats shined its flood light across the river to the bank and searched for movements. While the shore was still a good distance away, every now and then you could hear a screech and see a fast blur of movement on the docks among the wrecked boats. Brummer's boat, and fire team 2's boats would often have to stop and pull a body out of the water that was floating by. Every single one was already dead, most by brutal wounds. The corpses were already pale from blood loss and many were missing limbs or were simply torn open. Brummer would have to fight the urge to vomit on the spot when the occasional small child would be pulled from the water; at least that was what she assumed it was due to the size. Usually the remains were so violated that it was hard to believe it was even once a human. Finally, after boating through the carnage of what had once been the great New York City, the evacuation crew was approaching the civilian evacuation zone. Though the rest of the area was dark except for the fires, the evacuation zone, about a half a mile ahead of them, was lit up with lights and flares. The zone was a large dock, jutting out into the river below a large black top parking lot full of light posts still being run by generators. The sounds of the battle grew louder the closer the team got, sure to attract all the beasts the city could hold.

"Blue leader to USS Iwo Jima, we are nearing Evac zone." Brummer reported into the radio.

"Roger. Be careful out there Blue leader. HQ reports that the marines are being pushed back quickly." replied command on the Iwo Jima.

"Holy fuck, it sounds like a goddamn massacre out there." said DeSanta.

"More reason to get these civilians out fast." replied Brummer, but as she finished speaking there was a loud splash nearby. Fire team 2's boat stopped moving. Brummer stopped her boat as well and spoke over coms.

"Blue 5, why has your boat stopped?"

"Man overboard, Blue leader." the other boat replied.

"For fuck sake." mumbled Brummer. This was not the time for rookie mistakes. "Get their ass back in the boat. We have a mission to complete!" There was a pause and Brummer could see the confused movement of the other 3 men on fire team 2's boat.

"Ma'am, Blue 8. He's just. Gone." replied Blue 5 as everyone in the boat clicked on their helmet mounted flashlights and searched the water.

"What the fuck do you mean he's gone? Get him out of the water dammit!" exclaimed Brummer into coms. At this point she had driven her boat slowly over to them and her fire team began searching the water as well.

"I don't know! He just fell out of the boat and was gone! We can't find him!" replied Blue 5.

"Fuck!" Brummer said, now swapping coms to the marine boats behind them. "Green 1, I have a man overboard. Get those flood lights on the water and look for him."

Immediately, one of the larger SOC-Rs rumbled over to the RHIBs and a marine turned the large light toward the water and slowly panned over it.

"Blue leader, we aren't seeing shit." Green 1 reported.

"How the fuck docs a man disappear." Brummer said. This man overboard was a SEAL. Surely he wouldn't drown. She clicked on her flashlight and looked down into the water. The river was dark and littered with debris. The turbidity from all the dirt and rubble in it made finding a visual of this missing soldier difficult. Off of the coms, Brummer turned to her boat mates. "DeSanta, drop a flare into the water. Lets see if that helps us find him."

DeSanta pulled out the red tube from his utility vest and struck it. Burning red light erupted from the object and he dropped it into the water just below him. It sank slowly, lighting up the area below the boats. Brummer peered downward looking for the missing man. Just when she was starting to think there was nothing she saw something move past the flare as it fell, for just a split second. After that the flare went out.

"DeSanta, another." Brummer ordered as she looked down into the water with her light. This time she saw more movement. She saw something large moving just below the boat, but it was too large to be a man. Some form of aquatic life maybe? Whales were once known to enter the Hudson after all. "What the hell?" she murmured to herself.

"Dropping flare now, boss." DeSanta said as he struck the flare, igniting it. As he did this, Brummer's light shined onto a large glowing orb. It was a reddish color, and roughly the size of her head. She shined the light directly onto the object and the black center of it shrunk and pointed towards her. Then it hit her immediately and her stomach dropped. An eye.

"Oh fuck." she exclaimed. Before she could react, out of the water, behind DeSanta, a giant tentacle reached through the red illuminated darkness and wrapped itself around the unaware DeSanta's midsection.

"What the fu-!" DeSanta screamed as he was torn from the boat and dragged under water. Still holding the flare tight as he was pulled away, all that was seen was the illumination underwater and then sudden darkness as it disappeared; but it was far too early for the flare to go out.

"What the hell was that! Blue team, open up on that fucking thing!" Green 1 exclaimed over coms after seeing what had just happened. Brummer snapped out of the shock, cocked her MP7, and began unloading her magazine into the water below. The rest of the SEALs did the same. Water splashed all around the boats as bullets tore into the river from the 6 SEALs' weapons. After spending a magazine of ammunition each, every team member reloaded and searched the water in silence, looking for a what was most certain to be a dead beast.

"I think we got it. What was that." said Blue 6 over coms.

"Are there new threats that command didn't warn us about?" said Blue 3.

"It-It was an octopus. A giant fucking octopus." said Brummer in disbelief. She was the only one who got a clear look at the thing. "It must have been infected."

"Animals can be infected? Who was going to mention that shit!" said Blue 4.

"Well they sure as hell can now." said Brummer. She swapped coms again to the marine boats. "Green 1, are you seeing anything? I think we got that son of a bitch."

"We will circle the area and scout it out, Blue leader." Green 1 announced. The SOC-R rumbled forward slowly and circled the smaller boats. The flood light shined all around the area yet again and the marine gunners on board shined their flashlights over the sides. After about a minute of searching, Green 1 spoke over coms. "Well it's either gone or dead, we don't see a thing." There was a moment's pause and then the marine spoke again. "Wait a min-" Just then several of the monstrous tentacles shot out of the water and latched around the SOC-R.

"It's back! Open fire!" Brummer screamed as she took aim. The marines on board the SOC-R opened fire as well, trying to blast the tentacles off with their M240 machine guns.

"Get it off us!" yelled Green 1 as the octopus's head suddenly burst from the water. It tilted its head backwards, showing off its massive mouth and a pair of legs hung halfway out; presumably owned by DeSanta. The beast inhaled the remainder of the body and used its massive tentacles to rip the boat that it was holding in half. One marine was grabbed and shoved directly into the creature's mouth, screaming. Brummer watched as the man was shredded by the grinding teeth of the sea creature. The rest of the crew went flying with the boat debris to what she prayed was a quick and painless death.

"Open up!" yelled Green 2. The other boat sped forward, circling the beast as it opened up on it with its mounted minigun and side mounted M240s. Bullets tore into creature and it let out a low rumble of pain as the minigun blasted one of its limbs off.

"Take it out, take it out!" yelled Brummer as she and her team placed well aimed shots into the beast. She watched as flashes lit up the darkness from the 3 boats as they tried to take down the massive beast.

The octopus side-swiped one of its tentacles and swiped Blue 5 clean off of his boat with a loud smack. Then yet again the tentacle swiped back and grabbed Blue 4 from the boat, lifting him from his seat directly next to Brummer. It raised him into the air, screaming, as it squeezed, making the man into a red paste that plopped into the water below.

"Aim for its fucking head!" Brummer screamed to Green 2. They focused all of their fire onto the bulging red eyes of the beast. It rumbled again as chunks were torn from it and finally as one final burst from the minigun caught the creature in the eye, it went limp and splashed down hard into the water. It floated there for several moments before finally sinking down in a cloud of its own dark blood.

"What. The. Fuck." Green 2 said into coms. "Did we get it?"

"I-I think so." Brummer said. Just as she said that a message came over the radio from the Iwo Jima.

"Blue Leader, we are seeing gunfire from your position. Report."

"We came into contact with an infected-." she paused. "An infected octopus, sir." she knew how it sounded and was still trying to grasp what had just happened, herself. "We were not briefed on there being infected animals." There was a long pause and the Iwo Jima responded.

"We weren't aware of such threats, Blue Leader. This is news to us as well." There was another pause.

"We have lost 8 men and one of our boats. What are our orders?" again, there was a pause.

"Blue Leader, Command has been persistent in accomplishing this mission at all costs. Continue on."

"With all due respect, sir, we were short on space for civilians to begin with and are now down a boat." Brummer said, impatiently.

"Understood, Blue Leader. We sympathize for your losses but Command is being persistent. Continue as directed. Over and out." and with that closing statement, the radio went silent.

"God dammit! This Colonel in charge better know what the fuck he's doing, playing with lives like this!" Brummer yelled, and then threw a piece of boat debris out into the water. "Continue on mission. We need to get these people out."

The 3 remaining boats fired back up and continued towards the evacuation site, leaving the boat wreckage and dead beast behind. The site was just ahead a quarter of a mile and surely had seen and heard some of the fighting. As they approached the area and slowed down, they saw the urgency of the situation. Piled up, shoulder to shoulder, behind a chain link fence were over 100 civilians. Men, women, and children. On the other side of the fence were about 20 marines giving orders over a megaphone and standing watch on guard towers. Behind them were 3 men, assumed to be the senators. The sounds of fighting were very near now and just over the ridge at the end of the parking lot behind the dock, the flashes could be seen. The final stand was nearly over and the marines were losing. The boats all pulled up next to the docks and Brummer, and 2 marines unloaded. Ahead, a marine Captain approached.

"Its about damn time! We need to get these people the hell out of here!" yelled the Captain. "Our line is almost entirely pushed back and we aren't going to hold much longer!"

"Start loading them up, sir." Brummer replied. The Captain looked confused.

"This? This is it? How the fuck are we supposed to evacuate 123 people on 3 small ass boats?" the Captain roared. "Where are the fucking choppers? Where are the LAVs?"

"We are all there is, sir. Commands decision." Brummer replied.

"Jesus Christ. Lord help us all." the Captain said. "We need to load up as many people as we can and get them the hell out of here. Call the command and ask for reinforcements. We need more time!" Brummer grabbed her radio and called into the Iwo Jima.

"Blue Leader to the Iwo Jima. We have a situation here."

"What's going on over there, Blue Leader? Have you started evacuating?"

"Sir, we have 123 civilians here that need to go. Hostiles are about to overrun the position. We are requesting reinforcements or some choppers immediately." Brummer said quickly, as she gazed at the ridge and saw a flaming Humvee rolling backwards over the ridge with marines running back to the lot. After a few seconds the Iwo Jima responded.

"That a negative on request, Command will not authorize us to risk our last assets."

"Sir, these are people down here! There are children!" Brummer yelled.

"That's a negative Blue Leader. Command says priority evacuees are the senators. Then take anyone who doesn't risk their safety."

"Fuck their safety!" Brummer yelled as she threw the radio. "Who the fuck is commanding this god damn operation!" She turned to the two marines at her side and the Captain. "We need to get those fucking senators on first, and then load as many people as you can, starting with the children."

"Right." one of the marines said. "On it now."

Brummer looked to the ridge and saw that the marine line was now pushed back over the ridge to the edge of the parking lot. The civilian crowd began to scream and panic as the 20 marines at the gate rushed forward, through the fence, to join the fight. Humvees were blasting away at the rushing grey monsters with their .50 cal machine guns and a single Abrams tank was backtracking as it fired its main cannon into a swarm before being piled onto by the infected.

"I'll have my marines' hold these things back as long as we can. You get as many people out as you can." said the Captain as he charged his M16. "This will likely be the last you see of me and my men. Don't let this be a waste." The Captain then ran forward, gathering his men, and charged to the front line. As he left, the two boat marines ran back, escorting the 3 senators.

"Thank god! Get us the hell out of here now!" ordered one of the senators who was a fat, balding, white man in a clean suit. The fact he wore a perfectly clean suit among the mass of civilians covered in filth and blood said all that was needed to know about this man. Disgusting.

"As soon as we get the boats loaded up." Brummer replied.

"We don't have time! Those things are right there! We need to leave!" yelled the fat senator with a blonde, older woman next to him nodding in agreement.

"You work for these people. Now sit your ass down. I don't take orders from you, sir." Brummer said as Blue 3, Seaman Marko, grabbed the senators 1 by 1 and threw them down into the 2nd RHIB.

The two marines ran back to the fence and opened it up. The people rushed forward in a panic, knocking each other over, trampling one another.

"Children first!" yelled Brummer as the people pushed forward. They weren't listening. People began to dive onto the boats left and right, acting crazed. Brummer grabbed one man and tossed him back as he trampled a kid about the age of 10. She lifted the small girl and handed her over to Marko who placed her in their boat with 3 other children.

Brummer looked to the fight that was now halfway across the parking lot and moving fast to the docks. Thousands of the infected charged in waves against a couple of Humvees and a handful of marines. They had maybe a minute to get out of the area before it was completely overrun.

"Get back to the boats!" Marko yelled to Brummer and the 2 marines over the coms. Brummer looked around and saw that only about 20 people could actually fit onto the 3 boats with them without tipping them.

"We are staying behind. Let a couple more on, in place of us." Green 2 and Green 3 said. The two marines stepped away from the boats and fired upon the swarming infected now pushing towards the fence.

"It's been a pleasure, marines." Brummer said. "We have to go, now!"

The boats fired up and sped away from the docks, which were still full of people. Off the back of the SOC-R, two men had dived on and held on for dear life only to slip away into the water. People were jumping into the water to escape the docks now swarming with infection. Those who stayed were devoured. The worm-like parasites also swarmed the area and were plopping off of the dock and into the water, infecting the swimming civilians. Within seconds, everyone who wasn't on a boat was gone. Tears streamed down Brummers eyes as she watched the slaughter. She couldn't look away. In a way, she felt responsible. She felt bile rise up as a need to vomit overcame her, but she resisted. The same couldn't be said for Marko, who had vomited on his own lap in the boat.

"Blue Leader, report." Iwo Jima said over the radio. Brummer, exhausted, picked up the radio and responded.

"About 23 civilians evacuated. Docks were overrun." she took a breath. "Everyone else is KIA." A response came quickly.

"Command wants to know the status of the senators, Blue Leader."

Brummer couldn't believe it. All of the focus is on 3 people out of 120. She didn't answer.

"Blue Leader, respond."

She still didn't answer.

"Blue Leader, Command is pushing for an update. What is the condition of the senators?"

Before she could answer, a giant tentacle shot out of the water and flipped the 2nd RHIB, dumping the crew and everyone on it into the water. More tentacles rose up from the dark water and dragged people under, screaming, 1 by 1 till the screaming stopped. Brummer had no energy left to spend on this mission. She sat back on the boat as it kept speeding away from the city, placed her gun in her lap, and picked up the radio.

"Tell command their senators are all KIA. We are returning with 17 civilians. Heavy casualties. Blue leader, out." and with that she tossed the radio into the Hudson, closed her eyes, and fell asleep.

FIFTEEN

"USS Iwo Jima to Command. All 3 high value targets are KIA."

Miller's gut sank at the words and he looked around the room. LeBlanc slammed his fist on the table, Allen looked like a sad puppy as usual, and Hodge turned red in the face.

"What about the civilians?" asked Miller.

"Who the fuck cares about civilians! What do civilians matter in this! There are always more civilians. Those senators can't be replaced so easily! What a fucking disgrace!" screamed Hodge as he swiped all his papers off the table in front of him. Yet again, Miller held his tongue to keep the conversation shorter, but believed that Hodge was pushing the boundaries of treason at this point. The way he had handled this whole evacuation was pathetic and was the workings of a mad man.

"17 civilians made it out of the city. 2 of the 8 SEALs were left along with 2 of 8 marines." the officer on the Iwo Jima announced over the communication line.

"Good god. What have we done?" LaBlanc said, holding his head in his hands.

"It's a damn shame any of them made it back. They failed their nation and they failed me." Hodge said aloud, talking of course about the operators on the evacuation mission. This was too far. This was a comment that Miller couldn't take. He threw back his chair, stood straight up, and before he could let loose all of the things he had to say about Hodge, LeBlanc surprisingly beat him to it.

"Those were United States troops out there dying for these people! I can't believe you are saying these things!" Miller was stunned. Over the past few days, he hadn't seen LeBlanc do or say anything against Hodge's orders. He was a 'good soldier'.

"Check yourself, Major." Hodge growled.

"Absolutely not, sir. Time after time I have seen you play with people's lives and get them killed. You have no regard for any civilians or anyone under your own command! For 15 years I have served under you! For 15 years! But this-" he pointed at the UAV footage of the destroyed New York City "-This is too much!"

Hodge looked absolutely infuriated. LeBlanc's outburst caught him off guard and now the Colonel had officially lost his patience. He threw his chair back, leaned forward across the table, and pointed viciously at the major.

"You have officially lost your damn mind, son! Nobody speaks to me that way! Nobody! I am Colonel mother fucking Hodge. I was put in charge of New York's defense, not you! I hold all of the cards! This is your last chance to rethink the things you've said, and because of your 15 years of service, i'll pretend I never heard you say it!" Hodge yelled, staring down LeBlanc. Miller's mouth was hanging wide open. This whole argument was unexpected. LeBlanc leaned in closer over the table, making direct eye contact with Hodge.

"Fuck you, sir." he said sternly. Hodge's face was going from red to purple and his fists balled up so hard his knuckles went white.

"So be it." Hodge said through his teeth. "Corporal!" he yelled to the guard outside the room. One of Hodge's black armored personal troops quickly shuffled into the room holding an MP5. "Corporal, I want you to take Major LeBlanc here to the stockade and lock his ass up. Major, under my authority, you have been relieved of duty."

"You'll regret this, Hodge. You're going to get everyone killed." LeBlanc said as the Corporal cuffed his hands behind his back.

"We will see about that." Hodge said. He then turned away and faced the screen on the wall behind him showing the aerial bombing of New York City. The City lit up into several massive fireballs and clouds of debris blew all around as skyscrapers collapsed. "Miller, you are free to go. The doctor and I have some things to discuss and I don't need to be arguing with you next." Miller didn't say a word. He got up and left the command room.

Miller had hardly been out of the command room since arriving at the base. As he walked through the buildings of Fort Hodge he saw scenes of panic and despair. Everyone knew what was going on, how could they not? It was all over the news and many of them had lost numerous loved ones while they were stuck here doing nothing. Soldiers were slouched in the halls crying, many were preparing their weapons and gear, and some people were just pacing out of pure boredom. Hodge had a small army of trained troops and Special Forces at this fort but refused to use them. He had done nothing but sit by and watch the innocents die while he stockpiled the people who could save them. Miller walked out into the quad and headed towards the barracks, figuring that is where his friends would all be. He glanced to his left as he walked and saw LeBlanc being escorted by 3 black armored soldiers at gunpoint. A damn shame. The man was a good officer and was completely right about Hodge, but Hodge's time would come soon enough. Once General McCalister caught wind of Hodge and his fuck ups, he would be decommissioned for sure; but then again, Miller had heard no news of the General. It was almost like Hodge had cut communications with the man all together.

Miller stepped into the barracks and saw troops all over the place. Normally, they would be out spending their free time playing basketball or video games, but today everyone was sitting in their bunks in silence. He guessed video games about zombies and such felt too real all of the sudden. He looked over to his right as he came into the building and found just who he was looking for: John Rodriguez, with his and Miller's troops.

"That crazy bastard finally let you go, eh?" said John as he got up to shake Miller's hand.

"Yeah. And for that I am thankful." Miller said. "One more minute and i'd have to shoot the fucker." He wished that he was kidding.

"I think you'd do us all a favor, sir." said Hudson, who was playing a game of black jack on the bed with Edwards and Rookie, who appeared to have been kicking both of their asses.

"Yeah, well if it's not me, it might be LeBlanc." said Miller. "He was just relieved of duty and locked up." This got the attention of not only John and Miller's group, but the soldiers around them as well, who were now eavesdropping. This didn't bother Miller. The more who knew this, the better.

"You're joking." said John.

"Wish I was. You hear about New York City?" Miller asked. They all nodded.

"Heard they just finished evacuating lower Manhattan, and just in time too. Bombs just dropped." said Walt, who was listening to the radio broadcasts due to most television stations being down.

"Ha. Yeah, what an evacuation. It was a slaughter." Miller said, sitting down on the floor leaning against the bed. "123 people, and many troops defending them. 17 civilians and 4 troops made it back. Why? That fucker Hodge and his egotistical plans. People are guinea pigs to him and he is just a mad scientist."

"Good god. That's all?" John said quietly. They all could use a moral boost, and while this sure as hell wasn't it, they all needed to know the truth. The men around their group suddenly joined the conversation.

"Wait, are you saying Hodge was to blame for that? That son of a bitch. My cousin was down there. Last

I heard, she was waiting for Evac that never came. I haven't heard from her since that last call. You think she-" the man stopped talking and balled his fists as a tear streamed down his face.

"I'm sorry, man." Miller said, patting the man on the back.

"Yo, someone has to do something about this. I'm sick of being stuck in this base while millions of people are out there dying!" exclaimed another man. "My auntie was in Syracuse! They bombed the city!"

"I called my family and told them to get out of Albany while they still could. That was 2 days ago and Hodge blocked all outgoing communications! How am I supposed to know they are safe?" said another man. These 3 men had joined in with Miller's group now and were all invested in the conversation.

"The Major was the only one here who kept things in order while Hodge did whatever the hell he wanted, and now he is locked up! Most likely to get a court martial!" said the first man again.

"Something needs to be done before Hodge goes too far." said John.

"He already has." said Miller. "But I agree."

"If y'all need more help, then i'm your man. The name is Tyrice." said the second man.

"Same here, I'm Wong." said the last man.

"Hanks." said the first.

"Right. We will take all the help we can get." said Miller. He and his men all shook hands with the 3 soldiers.

"If we are really going to take him out of power we need to get the Major on board. He will be the next in command."

"I can probably get access to lock up to talk to him." said John. "But getting him out will be the tricky part."

"We can always get him out after. We just need him to be aware of the plan. With the General not coming to base any more, we need to take this into our own hands and fast." Miller replied.

"Whatever y'all decide, i'm in." said Tyrice. "I'm sick of being a bystander."

"Right. Well here is the plan. Once we fill in the Major, our only course of action is to rush the command room. Hodge is sure to be there with the doctor. Normally he has a couple of his personal guards around the room, but with the 10 of us, they would be smart to lay down their arms. I would put money on betting that his handful of guards are the only people left in this base that would defend him." Miller said. The other men nodded in agreement.

"And then we remove him of his command, disarm his guards, I think there were 8 of them total, and then we free the Major to inform the General. From there it is in fate's hands what happens to us. But I would rather go down for a failed coup than to sit by and watch this man murder more people." said John.

The rest of the men agreed with the plan and were eager to start it.

"We will take action first thing in the morning. Hodge usually gets into the command room around 0500. That will be the easiest time to get him. His personal guards are swapping shifts at 0530 so they will be paying less attention." Miller said.

"Get your gear ready for the morning, make any necessary preparations, and pray to god this works." John said.

<u>SIXTEEN</u>

Miller was backed into a corner at Facility 12, back in his dimension. His family was behind him, cowering in fear. Ahead of him was the entrance to the room which held the bridge. Their route to freedom. He had to get his family to that bridge, to safety. The world had ended and this was their only hope. Outside, the facility was surrounded by millions of swarming infected, waiting to tear apart his family and everyone else trying to escape. If they were caught, they would be brutally torn apart and devoured. Down the hall, Miller heard the gunshots of retreating troops who were covering the remaining civilians. As the shots stopped, the sound of screeching monsters grew louder and they came rushing down the hall running across the floor, climbing on the ceiling and walls, blood dripping from their gaping maws. Any men who tried to run from the swarm were engulfed and torn to ribbons of meat. Nothing could stop the swarm. Grenades were thrown till none were left and yet the swarm continued forward. Miller had to make a break for the door before it was too late, but he couldn't move. Ahead of him, people were being splattered onto the walls and ceiling as the swarm moved forward as one. Miller fired till his ammo ran out but it was no use. He still couldn't move.

"What do we do!" his wife cried. "What do we do!" He couldn't speak. He still couldn't move. He was paralyzed. "What do we do! Help us!" his wife continued

to cry, but still he could do nothing. The swarm was still surging forward. He closed his eyes awaiting death but it never came. It all went silent. He opened his eyes and the swarm was gone. He was back in his home, watching TV with his wife and daughters. Life was good and he was relieved.

"Daddy, I want popcorn." said his daughter to him.

"You just ate! You're still hungry?" he chuckled.

"Please daddy! Please!" his daughter said, giving him puppy dog eyes. He couldn't say no to that.

"Okay. I'll be right back." he said as he stood up from the couch and walked out into the kitchen. Outside, the sun was shining and neighborhood kids were out playing. A perfect day. He grabbed the bag of popcorn from the top shelf and headed back to the living room. "Okay! Who wants popcorn?" he said smiling, but his smile faded and he suddenly was in shock.

The living room was splattered with blood. It dripped from the ceiling onto the floor. The cushions on the couch were soaked like sponges, leaking out onto the floor. At his feet laid the severed head of his daughter. He looked to his left and his other daughter was halfway dragged into the floor vent leaving a trail of sticky blood behind from being dragged. His wife sat up and looked at him from the couch, covered in blood head to toe. The only space not covered in red was her eyes and mouth. She looked at him and spoke.

"Why didn't you save us. You said you would save us. You've doomed us. You've doomed THEM." she said.

Suddenly she was grabbed across the throat by a massive clawed hand. A large, scared, one eyed, infected man lifted her up and while she was still making eye contact, snapped her neck like a twig.

"No!" he screamed as he burst forward. He seemed to be moving at a snail pace across the room and wasn't making any progress. The beast turned at him, his wife's flesh hanging from its mouth, and screeched.

Miller awoke suddenly, grabbing his pistol, and raising it towards the air.

"Woah! Chill bro! It's me!" said Wong, jumping back from the weapon. Miller had been dreaming and was awakened by Wong, suddenly. He put the pistol away.

"Sorry, sorry. Bad dream." Miller said, bashfully. He was dripping sweat and felt like he had to vomit. The dream was so vivid.

"Yea bro, I can see that. God damn." Wong said. Next to him were Tyrice, Hanks, Rookie, and Edwards.

"That time already?" Miller asked. The men all nodded.

"The rest of the guys are all outside with the gear. We are just waiting on you, sir." said Rookie, handing Miller an M4. Miller grabbed the weapon, threw on his helmet, and stood up.

"Are you all ready for this? There is no going back." Miller asked.

"Honestly sir, I've been waiting for this asshole to get his for 3 years now. I'm happy to be a part of it." Tyrice said. Miller nodded.

The group left the barracks and headed out to meet the rest of the team. Sure enough, they had gathered up any armor, weapons, and ammo that they needed and had it stock piled outside.

"Glad you could join us, sir." said Hudson. Miller patted him on the back and looked around the group.

"Where is Sergeant Rodriguez?" Miller asked, noticing the man's absence.

"Not sure, sir. He left 20 minutes ago to talk to the Major and hasn't been seen since." said Walt.

"Shit. We may be compromised. We will have to move quickly without him and fast." said Miller. The thought that John had been captured and the plan was now known frightened the rest of the men, but it was now or never. If Hodge already knew, it was useless to call the plan off.

"Okay, let's move." said Walt. The group started to move across the quad when John finally came running to them from the command center, with Doctor Allen in tow. Miller felt sudden relief until he saw the look on John's face.

"Stop. Stop, something is wrong. Something is very wrong!" John said, panting, out of breath. "Something is happening."

"What are you talking about?" Miller asked, confused, as the rest of the group circled around. Doctor

Allen then made it over to the group. Panting, trying to catch his breath, he spoke between breaths.

"Hodge has gone too far this time, Miller! You have to do something!"

"What has he done? Did you talk to LeBlanc?" Miller asked.

"It's about LeBlanc! The Colonel has gone mad! After you left yesterday, we were talking about solutions to the bridge events and Hodge, he- well- he wants to weaponize the infected!" Allen said.

"What?" exclaimed Miller. "He can't do that!"

"Well he's trying. He has been experimenting on them for days now. First thing this morning I saw a chopper of his personal guards bring in a live specimen of one of those parasitic worms. You know, the ones that infect people. I went to talk to LeBlanc and Hodge's guards are all over the damn place. I couldn't get in. I think- I think that they are going to test the infection on the Major." John said, panting and wiping his forehead.

"That crazy mother fucker!" exclaimed Hanks.

"Where are they now? Allen, where the fuck are they?" Miller asked, grabbing both of the doctor's shoulders.

"Well, they would need a place to contain him if they were to infect him, so, I suppose the logical place to go would be lockup." Allen said with a shaky voice.

"New plan boys, we need to get into lockup before Hodge's plan goes any further." Miller said. The rest of the men were all in agreement. They headed toward the stockade, ready for a fight if need be.

As they walked across the main lawn, nearing the stockade, they were met by several of Hodge's personal guards, who were fully geared up carrying M4s.

"You men have reason to be carrying those weapons on base like that?" asked the Sergeant in charge of the black armored men. The same Sergeant that had locked up John and his men when they first arrived at the base days ago after losing Facility 12.

"We need to get in to see Major LeBlanc." said John.

"No can do. LeBlanc has been relieved of his rank and is not to be spoken to. Hodge's orders. Turn around and go back to the barracks." the Sergeant said.

"We aren't requesting anything here. We need to see LeBlanc and that's final." said Miller, stepping up to the Sergeant. The man did not look impressed.

"You may outrank me, Miller, but you don't outrank Hodge and his orders stand. Now back the fuck up before you all end up in lockup with LeBlanc!" the Sergeant yelled. He began to lift his rifle to aim at Miller but as he began, Miller swung the stock of his own rifle across the face of the Sergeant, knocking him out cold and dropping him to the ground. The men aside the Sergeant were in shock and before they could raise their rifles to fire, Wong and Rookie had tackled them to the ground as well.

"Zip tie their hands and lets move. We need to clear out the building and get to LaBlanc." John ordered. Hanks did so and as one man rolled over to yell for help, Hudson kicked him across the chin, knocking him out. "Move in." John ordered.

To their surprise, the stockade was not very well guarded. The building was empty and it was perfectly quiet. The only sounds were their footsteps and the rattling of their gear. The 10 men moved in unison through the halls, clearing each room and cell as they went.

"Where the fuck is everyone?" whispered Rookie.

"Something isn't right, here. Hanks, Wong. You two post out here while we clear the last block." Miller ordered. The two men set up shop in the hallway and kept their guns facing the entrance.

The rest of the men moved into the last block and right away, something was off. The normal smell of dusty concrete now smelled of rotting meat and sour breath. Just ahead they heard heavy breathing and growling. The sound of something hard scraping across metal bars is what really got their attention. They already knew what it was but nobody wanted to admit it. They approached the final cell of the block and Miller had to take a deep breath before looking.

Miller looked around the corner into the cell and was immediately let down. Staring back at him within the cell was a man who was clearly infected. He wore a military uniform, drenched with blood down the front. His skin was greying, but not fully grey, showing he was recently infected. The face was beginning to alter due to the changes the parasite brings, but the name tag on the uniform made any further questions answered. "Major LeBlanc."

"Son of a bitch. We are too late." Miller said to the men as they all approached and looked at the sickly man. Beside the man were piles of torn and devoured flesh, unrecognizable.

"God damn it! Hodge is going to pay when we find him!" John yelled. "And is that sick fuck feeding him? Are those bodies?"

"Who the hell did he feed to it?" Alan said, as he turned and vomited down the concrete wall.

Suddenly shots rang out from within the facility. The sounds of a firefight. There was a loud bang, 2 more shots, and then silence.

"Tyrice, Alan. Go check it out! Carefully." ordered John.

The two men approached the door and as they got ready for a breach, the door swung open, striking Alan across the face, knocking him to the ground. Two black armored men entered and fired several shots into Tyrice's chest. The full metal jacket rounds tore out his back and he fell to the floor in a pool of his own blood.

"Shit! Take cover!" yelled John as he fired 3 rounds back at the attackers and dove behind the cover of a brick wall inside a cell. Several more shots rang out and Alan was put down for good. Hudson took a round to the knee, dropping him to the floor screaming. Bullets pinged off of the wall behind them as more black armored men entered the room.

The men remaining in Miller's team dove into a nearby office and fired back out the window, hiding behind desks and cabinets. John let loose a burst of fire from his M4 and caught one of the entering attackers in the stomach, splattering his guts onto the wall behind him.

"They've got us pinned!" yelled Rookie, who pumped his shotgun and blasted a soccer ball-sized chunk out of the wall next to the door.

Hudson was still in the middle of the firefight, rolling around on the ground, unable to stand. He was screaming in agony as the bullets whizzed by overhead.

Brass casings clinked off of the concrete floor as more and more shots rang out. Dust fell from the walls as bullets collided with them. Miller sat up and fired a full auto burst from his rifle at the enemies. His shots were well aimed, as they cut across the wall and went into the throat of another attacking soldier. The man slumped down the wall as his head fell to his chest.

"There is no way out! What do we do!" yelled Edwards, whose rifle jammed. He was now using his sidearm. Just as he asked that, something flew out into the middle of the cell block and clanked around on the ground as it rolled. John saw it first.

"Flash-bang!" he yelled as he dipped his head and covered his ears. The loud bang echoed off of the concrete walls and anyone who didn't cover their eyes were blinded.

Miller's ears were ringing but he could still see. Dizzy, he sat up and saw 6 black armored soldiers in the cell block aiming guns at Miller's group as they hid behind cover. He looked over at John, and saw that John was in the same state. Rookie and Edwards were laying down clutching their ears, while Walt was aimed at the assaulting troops. While the two groups were in a stand-off, a 7th member of the assaulting force strolled in through the door. Hudson was still on the ground screaming, rolling around. The newcomer walked up to Hudson, pointed the barrel of his pistol at his head, and pulled the trigger. A shot rang out as Hudson's brains were splattered onto the concrete. This newcomer was none other than Hodge, himself.

"Gentlemen. You have put me in a tough place!" announced Hodge.

"Fuck you, you crazy bastard!" yelled John.

"Am I crazy? Following a losing system, investing all your resources in the weak, and being compliant with losing tactics is what is crazy! Am I crazy? I just don't think so! I like to think of myself as a leader! I'm going to save us all!" Hodge yelled, with a crazed smile on his face. "When my grandson first died to these things I was distraught! What a waste of a good soldier! When city after city fell in just a few short days I was infuriated. What a waste of good resources! But now, now I can see the path to victory!"

"The path to victory is sacrificing your own men to make monsters? Leaving the civilian population to die?"

Miller said. "That sounds like the work of a madman, Hodge!"

"LeBlanc was no longer my man. He was a traitor, and he got the punishment of a traitor. And now I can use him to fight these monsters to save the civilians! Can't you see? I have made him stronger! The man is a better killer than you will ever be!" Hodge exclaimed.

"Who the hell did you feed to him you crazy fuck?" yelled Walt, who still had his sights on the nearest enemy's head. Hodge laughed.

"Miller, when was the last time you've checked on your people?" Hodge asked. Miller had been so wrapped up in work over the past few days that he hadn't had time to. The realization hit him like a brick.

"You-you-" Miller couldn't get the words out.

"You sick bastard! They were civilians! They were all that was left!" Edwards exclaimed, his hearing just coming back.

"They were all that was left from a diseased and twisted world. A reminder of what happens when you fail. You two, and all those people brought this plague upon us and now you'll repent for it!" Hodge yelled. "I fed them to my new creation and they fueled his ability to kill. They are a part of him now and will help me save us all!"

"You sick fucker! Some of those were children! Where are the rest of them?" yelled Miller. He was crying now. Tears were streaming down his face and he was grinding his teeth in rage. Edwards, too, was curled up on the floor rocking back and forth, now knowing that they were the only two left from their world.

"You think I would keep the rest around to bother my progress? I had them executed last night while you slept. If it eases your pain, just know that they were sleeping too. I'm not a monster, after all." Hodge said, firmly.

"You fuck! I'm going to kill you! I'm going to kill all of you!" screamed Miller as he pulled the trigger and let out a full auto spray from his rifle, cutting down another one of the black armored men. Walt did the same, followed by John, and the firefight again, started.

"None of you will leave here alive! You can't stop progress. I am in control!" yelled Hodge as he fired a pistol back at Walt, striking him in the shoulder. He flew backwards to the ground with a yelp.

"I'm hit but I'm good!" Walt yelled, as he struggled to lift his M4 back up to his shoulder.

"It's been a pleasure, gentlemen. I'm sorry for everything I've brought down upon you." Miller yelled to the others as he ran out of ammo and swapped to his last magazine on his pistol. He dropped his rifle to the floor, which was now coated with brass casings, specs of blood, and concrete chunks. In one last burst of bravery he leapt out from behind cover and took aim with his pistol; but before anyone could respond, a loud, high pitched siren started outside.

"What the hell is that?" asked Rookie. The fighting stopped, all men stood still and the room was silent.

Suddenly dust shook from the ceiling as an explosion rattled in the distance and the pops of small arms fire sounded outside the building.

"It's here." said John. They had prepared for this moment. They knew it was coming and the time was now.

"All hands report to battle stations! A bridge has opened outside of Fort Hodge!" a man yelled over the loudspeaker outside.

"Grab the specimen and get the chopper ready! It's time to go!" yelled Hodge to his men as they caught what used to be LeBlanc with a catch pole and rushed the screeching creature out of the block. "I'd love to finish this fight myself, boys, but I will let the bridge do the rest." With that last comment, Hodge and his men left the stockades to evacuate.

"We can't let him get away!" yelled Edwards, who was rushing the exit, stepping over all of the bodies littering the floor.

"Let him go. We have bigger things to worry about now, like getting everyone on this base out of here." Miller said. Edwards turned to argue but Miller cut him off. "His time will come, and he will pay." With that, Edwards ran over to help Walt up, who was bleeding from his shoulder wound. The hollow point round that had hit him had blown a gaping hole in his flesh, rendering his one arm useless.

The remaining 5 men left the building, walking past the bodies of Hodge's men as well as their own. They passed the 3 men who had volunteered to help them and were rewarded with death in an ambush. The stockade was a mess. Hodge would pay. The men continued on and stepped outside into chaos. Everywhere, soldiers were running to the wall defensive positions and vehicles were deploying outside of the wall.

"Here they come!" yelled a soldier in a guard tower as he opened up with his M240 machine gun. A new battle was starting, and this one could be their last.

"Let's end this shit." said Miller to John, who nodded in agreement.

<u>SEVENTEEN</u>

"Everyone clear the tarmac and keep moving forward! Please keep order!" yelled the military officer to the crowd. Jessica moved along with them after stepping off of the cargo bay of a Chinook helicopter. Just a few days prior, her life had been turned upside down when a bridge event brought her city of Syracuse to the ground. She was lucky to have escaped when she did. The city, as well as anyone left alive in it, was turned to ash when the military strategically bombed it. It didn't help, of course. No matter how many of the creatures were killed in the explosion, more and more bridge events happened, and all over the world too. After barely escaping Syracuse with her life, she was escorted with a small group of other survivors to a small refugee center set up outside of Philadelphia, Pennsylvania. After only having been there a couple of short days, more bridges had opened inside the city and it then shared the same fate as New York City and Syracuse. Battles fought, battles lost, and the city was turned to ash. An emergency evacuation of the refugee camp was set into motion and now all of the civilians from that camp were moved to a new one.

Jessica was now deep into the Appalachian Mountain range in the wilderness of West Virginia. The site of this new camp was said to be an old cold war bunker, able to withstand a nuclear war. Anyone inside could run the east coast in safety, and that's just what they did. After learning of the morally destroying news that the entirety of Washington D.C. was the site of several bridge events, all decisions for the east coast came from this facility. It was unknown if the president and his cabinet were alive. Contact with them had been lost nearly 26 hours ago, and UAV drone footage had shown the city to be a wasteland, overrun by the very beasts that destroyed it.

"Please follow the directions of the soldiers assisting you. Stay together and please remain calm." said the military officer again. The man stood in a watchtower near the tarmac speaking through a megaphone to the group of 50 civilians unloading from the choppers. Jessica followed the group off of the landing pads and into the fenced-off area. All around her were sobbing and filthy people, armed soldiers, and trees. So many trees. It was a change from the past few days. Behind her, helicopters were landing and taking off constantly, bringing new refugees and taking away squads of soldiers to go rescue more. It was a high traffic area.

"Excuse me ma'am, please move forward to the tents. Someone will assist and direct you from there." said a young soldier to Jessica. He had fresh cuts on his dark face and his uniform was dirty. It appeared the young man was fresh out of a combat zone and now here to assist the civilians. This appeared to be the case with most of the troops here, showing that man power was running low. Jessica followed the man's instructions and headed into the olive canvassed tents at the end of the fenced area. People were constantly coming through the station and splitting off to different areas.

"Step forward." said a young woman working the receiving table inside the tent. Just like the other man, she looked tired and beaten. Her camouflage uniform even had a spec of blood on it. "What's your name, ma'am?" asked the woman in a monotone voice. This was routine for her.

"Jessica Richmond." Jessica replied. People around her were shaking and terrified, but she tried to keep her composure.

"Jessica, do you have any skills that could be useful for us? What was your career?" the attendant asked. Jessica answered quickly.

"I, uh, I was a nurse." The attendant quickly perked up.

"Like, at a hospital? You have medical experience?" she asked again.

"Yes. I worked in the emergency room at a hospital." Jessica replied sheepishly. The attendant grew a slight grin and shuffled through her forms.

"Perfect. We are in some serious need of medical personnel around here. We have a few doctors and a handful of medics but more help is needed." the attendant handed Jessica a form and continued speaking. "This is paperwork for the directory. I need you to continue to the right and give this to the man attending the medical tents."

Jessica looked down at the forms but was told to move on quickly. She didn't have a chance to read them. As she walked she looked behind her. Most of the other refugees were being sent to the left to the bunks, while she and the injured were being sent to the medical camp. Before she could even question what was going on, she had reached the attendant the previous woman had spoken of.

"What's your injury?" said the tall man in blue camouflage behind the table. His cap was pulled low so she couldn't see his face and he sounded annoyed.

"I-Im not injured." replied Jessica. Before she could explain the man spoke up in an even more annoyed tone.

"If you're not injured you have no need to be here. Every minute you waste here is a minute taken from a patient and I've seen too many dead civilians today." the man stood up from his chair and went to shoo her away.

"I was told to give this form to you." Jessica said, handing forward the paper. The man paused, reached across the table and took the form. He examined it and just like the woman before, he smiled and relaxed a bit.

"Welcome to the army. You have been drafted as a triage medic. You will be working under me." Jessica paused and was in shock. The man continued. "I am First Lieutenant Avery, I will be your commanding officer here", he looked down at the sheet and looked back up, "Private Richmond."

"I-I-" Jessica was struggling to speak. All composure she had was now gone.

"Miss, I am aware how this is shocking news to you, but we need you and we need you now." Avery said.

He grabbed a uniform out of a box under the table and turned back. "Take this. This will be your uniform. Later today we will get some dog tags and patches made for you, but right now I need you to put this on and report back to me." Jessica took the uniform and looked back up at him.

"I'm no soldier." Jessica said quietly. Avery smiled.

"It'll be okay. I'm not asking you to do any fighting. I'm asking you to do what you did before all of this. Help people." he said. Jessica went to protest but her husband's final last words ran through her head.

"Make me proud."

And she would. She nodded and followed orders. She would save lives and make her husband proud.

—

"Patient has a cut across her face. It appears deep. We need to get this closed up ASAP before she bleeds out." Jessica stated as she peeled back the blood drenched gauze from a woman's face.

"The man with her said that an infected slashed her before troops picked her up. She's lucky to be alive." said the man next to her, Private Eldrige.

Eldrige was an army medic who had survived the fight in Philadelphia and was lucky enough to make it here with Jessica. Although she had only been here for 5 hours or so now, she had already learned so much. She had learned that 'here' was actually known by the military as

Eagle Point. As she knew already, it was the command center for the US military's east coast operations, and was being run by a General. He called the shots while the American government was missing in action. She had learned that it was no exaggeration that resources were being run dry. She had started working right away after being drafted and was already exhausted at the number of wounded coming through the lack of medical staff. As if this all wasn't already bad enough, she also learned that in the west, the terrorists were staging more and more attacks. They used the bridge events as a distraction so they could make moves, and those moves were getting closer and closer to them.

"She is going to need a dose of morphine and many stitches now, or she is going to code." said Jessica to Eldrige. This woman was on the verge of shock and needed help now.

"I'll take care of her. You just move on to another patient." Eldrige said. Jessica turned and moved across the tent to another bed which had a man on it who was missing a leg up to the thigh. Strands of tendon hung from the wound and blood squirted onto the table. The man was out cold from shock and morphine, and Avery was working on the wound with another medic.

"I need a tourniquet on his thigh now or he is going to die!" Avery ordered. The other medic ran around the table.

"I don't even know how he has lasted this long." said the medic. "What did they say did this to him?"

"A fucking infected decided to make a snack of his leg. Stripped it of meat like a chicken wing. Our boys managed to grab him for Evac before it could finish him." Avery said. The man suddenly jolted awake and began screaming and flailing.

"Oh shit! We are gonna need some help. Eldrige! Get the hell over here!" yelled the medic. Eldrige, who had just finished patching up the other woman ran over and held the man to the table.

"What can I do?" asked Jessica. Avery looked up at her and spoke, wincing as a stream of the wounded man's blood squirted onto his cheek.

"Richmond, we are going to need some more morphine for this man, pronto. We have more stashed away in the command building's lab. Go grab that for a reserve supply. And be quick about it!" Jessica took off running.

As she ran she saw more and more beds of wounded civilians. Some fine, others not so fine. Around the corner of the building was a pile of black, human sized bags and in those bags were the people who really were not fine; and unfortunately there were more than she cared to count. Wearing her blood stained uniform, she burst through the doors of the command building and a soldier stopped her.

"Woah woah woah. I'm gonna need to see some ID there, sweetheart." said the soldier, hand on his sidearm which was holstered to his hip.

"Private Jessica Richmond, US Army. I'm- well- I'm new. As of today." Jessica said. The man smiled and eased up.

"Well Private, I don't see any identification. Mind telling me who sent you?" the man asked. He was wasting precious time that the patients did not have. Annoyed, she answered.

"Lieutenant Avery sent me. We need more morphine supplies quickly." The man didn't seem convinced. Annoyed, she continued. "Tall black man, mustache, medical division. Do I go on or should I call him over and waste more of his time?"

"No no. No need for that, thank you. Jesus Christ lady, you're a temperamental one, eh? Go on." the man said as he stepped aside. "Just make it fast. Command is making moves in there. Something big is going down."

Jessica continued through the building, following signs for medical storage. Just as she expected, she found it. The storage was a closet in the lab packed with materials. Unfortunately most were things they didn't need. There was gauze, wraps, tapes. These were all good things to have in stock, but what they needed more was medicine and painkillers. She searched and found what she was looking for. Morphine. The last of the morphine supply. She gulped in fear that they would soon run out. Thinking of the new wounded that came in day after day that would have a lesser chance of survival scared her. Closing the door, she exited the lab.

As she moved down the hallway towards the exit of the building, she was shoved aside by a radio operator who then burst into the doors of the command center next to her. The young man was certainly in a hurry, and was wasting no time. She could only imagine the amount of transmissions for help that this man had been dealing with the past few days. Curiosity got the best of her and she crept over next to the now open door and listened.

"Sir! We just had a call for Evac from some place called Fort Hodge. They say that they are under siege and need helicopter support quickly. They said they have over a hundred troops stationed there, and many of which are Special Forces and their commanding officer has gone AWOL. We could most certainly use those personnel here and for more runs out into the infected zones. The only issue is that I can't find any evidence of such a fort." exclaimed the radio operator. Next another, much older man, calmly spoke. Jessica heard him sit up from his chair, which he was no doubt sitting in, looking over military and evacuation plans. All of the high ranking officials here had been extremely busy.

"Ah, Ghost Town. That is because it formally does not exist, Corporal. I assure you that it is there, though. Looks like I have found why Colonel Hodge has gone radio silent. Have them radio in their coordinates and send whatever they say they need. We need those soldiers back here, safe and sound. Get it done, now."

Jessica turned and headed away from the door back to the medical tent with the supplies. The last thing she heard before leaving was the radio operator say over his headset, "Mission is a go. General McCalister has given us the green light."

EIGHTEEN

The base was now full of the sounds of war as men and women opened fire on the assaulting wave of beasts. As soon as the bridge appeared, Miller had directed one of the radio operators to call for evacuation to General McCalister. Now that Hodge was no longer in charge, the call was easy to make.

"Fort Hodge, be advised. The closest birds to you will take an hour to reach you." said the operator on the other end of the radio.

"We will try to hold out till then, command." replied the radioman, Corporal Ackerman.

"We will, however, have an Apache gunship to support you in 40 and are watching via drone." said command.

"Much appreciated. Fort Hodge, out." Ackerman said as he ended the conversation. He turned to Miller, who had wounded Walt in tow. "What are my orders, sir?"

"I need you and the rest of your staff to stay here to keep an open line of communications as needed." said Miller. Ackerman nodded.

"What about me, Miller. I'm not out of this yet." said Walt, holding his glock, with his other arm in a bloody sling.

"Walt, I need you to keep security here in case they break through." Miller replied. Walt nodded. "Rodriguez, Rookie, Edwards, and myself will all be outside directing the defense. We need to hold out until rescue comes."

Outside, the sounds of explosions and the chatter of machine guns rang out over the open valley floor. "Make sure these choppers show or we are all dead."

Miller sprinted down the hallways of the command center and crashed through the front doors of the building with his shoulder. He charged his M4 and ran over towards John and the others. John was up on the walkway at the top of the concrete wall, popping off shots in semi-automatic out into the swarm. Next to him, Edwards did the same while Rookie manned a mounted M240 and blasted bursts of fire out into the valley. Miller ran up the stairs and joined them on the walkway, where he instantly had his stomach drop. Across the valley floor from Fort Hodge's outer fence was a massive blue portal unloading tens of thousands of the creatures. The hordes charged across the open fields towards the fences as soldiers fired upon them.

"The valley floor is covered in anti-personnel landmines and we have M2 .50 caliber machine guns mounted in the gunnery towers on the wall. The mortar teams are setting up right now, but we need support." As John said this, several of the landmines went off, sending chunks of gore wide into the air.

"A gunship is 40 minutes out and we have command radioing in enemy movements as they watch with a drone. Other than that, we need to hold out till Evac comes in an hour." Miller said as he fired a burst into a smaller infected that got ahead of the swarm and leapt onto the outer fence. It slipped and fell to the ground.

"An hour! We will all be dead in an hour!" exclaimed Rookie as he blasted into the horde.

"We can make it. We need to." said Miller. He thought back on the many battles he survived with these things. "I've done this before. We will survive."

A dull thud sounded, followed by several more and explosions blasted the middle of the horde, leaving red and black craters in the ground.

"Mortars are up!" yelled John.

"Hallelujah!" yelled Edwards.

The mortar fire kept up at a steady pace and land mines kept exploding, but with every explosion, new swarms came crashing through the smoke.

"It looks like they are going to circle around us! They can't make it to the fence but they will try to surround us! John, I need you to head to the east side of the base and make sure those .50's are up and firing." yelled Miller. John took off running to do just that.

"What about the main horde? What are we going to do?" asked Edwards. He dropped a magazine from his M4 and slapped a new one home as he spoke. On the floor around him were 2 more magazines. The men were pissing through ammunition and the battle had just began.

"We need a distraction of some sort." Miller said as he looked around. He then spotted 4 Humvees and an LAV sitting at the vehicle bay below the wall. He grabbed one of the soldiers running by. "Private, are those vehicles battle ready?"

"Yes sir! Just awaiting orders." said the soldier, perking up. "Are we taking the fight to them?"

    "Oh we are going to sure as hell try!" said Miller. "Get the crews for those vehicles ready!"

"Yes sir!" yelled the soldier as he ran off.

"We are going to take that convoy out there and try to buy some time." said Miller. As he said this, the crews ran to the vehicles and began loading into them. Miller joined them. "Hold the walls. I will be back."

Miller ran down to the vehicles and climbed aboard the mounted MK-19 grenade launcher on one of the Humvees.

"Joining us, sir?" asked the soldier from before, who climbed into the driver's seat.

"Wouldn't miss it." said Miller as he cocked the launcher.

—

John ran through the quad, telling any idle troops to follow him to the east wall. He had gathered about 8 men with him by the time he got there. There were only 10 other men on the wall when he arrived and the fight had just began.

"Who is in charge over here, Corporal?" asked John once he got up to the wall. The Corporal was shaking with tears in his eyes. He couldn't have been older than 18.

"Y-you are, s-sir." said the boy. His rifle rattled in his hands as he spoke. John felt sympathy for the man, but they needed every able-bodied man fighting.

"Okay! Listen up! This wave is going to try to get over our walls. We are the only thing stopping that from happening!" John said. He looked at the young man. "Corporal! I need you to get it together and get in that gunnery tower! Can you do that?"

"Yes sir." the man said, wiping tears from his eyes. He climbed into the tower and seconds later the heavy, boom boom boom, of the M2 began firing into the oncoming swarm.

"The rest of you need to keep up the fire until support arrives! Man those mounted M240s! I need someone to be a runner for ammo!" ordered John to the group. Another man volunteered and took off back to storage. The rest of the men kept up the defense.

John took aim on top of the wall and took precise shots at the targets that appeared to be the biggest threat. He peered down the scope mounted to his rifle and looked out to the swarm. It was significantly smaller than the original horde, but there were still at least 1000 of the infected running to the fences. An infected person jumped onto the fence and began climbing. John fired two rounds into its chest and the beast flew back off of the fence. After that came another, and another. Next thing he knew, the first fence was crawling with climbing creatures. They took round after round and some were sliced and caught in the razor wire, but they kept coming, and the bodies were mounding in front of the fence. Below the concrete wall, two soldiers were running through the gates towards the horde mounding just outside the first fence.

"What the fuck are they doing?" asked John.

"They are sappers, sir. They are going to rig the fence to blow once the horde is too large." replied the Sergeant next to him.

Seeing the fence begin to shake as the weight of the beasts loosened the foundation, John yelled for the men to come back. They didn't hear him. The two men worked quickly just behind the fence setting up their explosives as the fence wobbled more and more.

"Get out of there! It's coming down!" yelled John. It was no use. As he did so, another group of the beasts slammed full speed into the fence and it gave way. The fence toppled over. The first sapper was the lucky one. The fence and the weight of the beasts pinned his legs to the ground and the razor wire on top had slit open his neck. In a matter of seconds the man bled out. The second man wasn't so lucky. He turned to run and the infected had grabbed his feet out from under him.

The man screamed in agony as he was dragged backward into the mass and disappeared under them. All that was heard was his screams through the gunshots as he was torn to shreds. Within seconds the infected were through the first fence and mounding up on the second.

John snapped back to reality and fired his rifle once again. They were going to get through. There was no way that they wouldn't. As he fired, the second fence collapsed as well. If they got through the third, all that was left was the wall, which they could easily scale with their clawed hands and feet. Just when all seemed lost, hope came rolling past the perimeter. The convoy was out and drawing the creatures away.

—

Miller blasted round after round out of the MK-19 into the swarm, assaulting the east wall. The grenades he fired erupted in flashes of orange and yellow as they exploded in the masses of infected. Limbs and gore flew all over the place, painting the green grass red with the blood of the enemy. The Humvee he was in sped past the group, trailed by 2 others, which also lit up the swarm. As they drove past, the swarm shifted its attention from the hard-to -reach food atop the wall, to the readily available food out in the field. They quickly jerked around and all began to sprint after the vehicles.

"Team 3, I need you to keep those fuckers off of our asses." Miller spoke into his mic to the Humvee in the rear. Its M2 boomed as its BMG rounds tore infected in half.

"On it, boss." replied the gunner.

"Team 1, take us further out into the field. We will link up with the other convoy." Miller ordered the first vehicle. The driver pressed his foot hard on the pedal and the vehicle took off at amazing speed. As fast as they were going, the creatures kept pace. All around them, the grey bodies were sprinting and diving after the trucks.

"Damn these fuckers are fast!" yelled team 3's gunner. Miller looked behind him and saw that the beasts were only a couple meters from the Humvee. In his fascination with the speed of things, he was distracted and missed the ones charging from the side.

"Shit! Keep them off of us!" yelled Team 1's driver as several of the beasts slammed full speed against the side of their vehicle. The beasts hit face first into the windows and smeared their faces down the side. Although they killed themselves, they helped the horde. The Humvee rocked, went up on two side tires and slammed back down. The massive jolt of force knocked the top gunner loose as he tumbled out of the truck's top hatch. The driver continued driving on, not noticing. He was preoccupied with the swarm around him, close enough now to scrape the vehicle with their claws.

"Watch out!" yelled Miller to his driver. The gunner from Team 1's truck stood up off the ground as Miller's truck barely missed him. As the Humvee swerved around the man, he was tackled to the ground by several infected that tore ribbons of flesh from him that flew through the air like gory streamers. As Team 3's Humvee passed by him, his blood splattered the windshield.

"Fuck! I can't see!" yelled Team 3's driver over the coms. His windshield wipers were on but the gore just smudged around. "I can't see! They are all over!" yelled the driver again as he floored it across the field. The Humvee ran down several infected as he drove, making serious speed bumps. Gore splattered the Humvee as the driver was still blinded as to where he was going.

"Watch out!" yelled the gunner just before the vehicle slammed into a tree. The front of the truck crumpled as the driver flew through the windshield and landed out on the grass. Before he could get up, a group of infected swarmed him and began to devour him. The gunner, who was shaken and confused, still stood in the hatch of the vehicle. As what was going on came back into focus, he spun the M2 in all directions, blasting infected as they circled. They closed in all around him as he shot wildly. Hundreds of them climbed the vehicle all around him.

"Go back for him!" yelled Miller to the driver as they drifted around a tree and Miller let a few more rounds fly into the swarm. They headed back for the stranded man but saw they were too late.

"Help me! Help me!" the man cried over coms as the creatures crawled on top of the vehicle and clawed at him. All that Miller could see after that was the man's upper half come free from his waist and get dragged into the feeding frenzy. His lower half tumbled back into the truck.

"Shit! We need to get to the other convoy now!" yelled Miller as their truck and Team 1 sped back towards the front of the base, with thousands of infected following. A couple hundred of them remained to assault the walls, but John and his men were able to defend.

As Miller's convoy sped back around to the front of the base, they drove right into a massive warzone. All over the place, bodies were laying. Small and large arms fire shot out into the field from the walls and explosions rocked the ground. Miller had some second thoughts about driving out here, but realized that all of the landmines would be gone by now. Thousands among thousands of the beasts still charged forward.

"Convoy 2, where the hell are you?" cried Miller over the coms as his convoy ran down some straggling infected.

"Coming now, boss." replied Team 4. Just then the massive LAV came driving around the west corner of the base tailed by another swarm of infected. The distraction plan worked, but how much time it bought them was uncertain. "We lost Team 5 back there. They are gone."

The LAV drove through crowds of infected, squashing them like bugs underneath it. The large 25 mm cannon fired at the large groups while its M240s kept the stragglers off of the sides.

"Let's bring these hordes away from the walls and further out into the valley, boys." said Miller over coms. He was answered with a "Roger" from the 2 other teams. The LAV, tailed by the 2 Humvees, took off away from the base with thousands following it. "Man we are lucky these things are easy to distract." said Miller to his driver.

"Let's hope it stays that way, sir." said the Private.

The 3 vehicles took up an arrowhead formation away from the base, with the LAV taking the lead.

"Looks like we have this in the bag fellas!" said the driver of the LAV over the coms. He spoke too soon. Although they had managed to get a good distance away from the swarm, they weren't safe.

Miller's Humvee suddenly slammed down into a crater from a mortar round and the entire truck went into a roll. Miller fell back into the truck and was tossed around the inside like he was inside a maraca. The truck flew through the air, slammed into the ground, rolled over 3 times and came to a stop on its side. He was dazed.

"Daddy, why did you let us die? Why did you let it get us daddy." said Miller's daughter to him. She was covered in her own blood and her white dress was drenched and dripping.

"Why did you let it get us, Steve? Why didn't you help us?" said his wife, whose neck was snapped to the side, unnaturally. He remembered all too well how the massive beast had killed her.

They all stood in front of him, outside of the toppled truck, standing in the grass. They spoke together.

"It killed us. Why did you let it happen? Why?"

His wife leaned into his face and spoke to him in a deep voice.

"You need to wake up Miller."

"You need to wake up, Miller!" yelled the Private as he climbed through the flipped Humvee back to him. "Wake the fuck up!"

Miller snapped awake. He looked around and was dizzy.

"What happened?" he asked, confused. His earpiece then screamed at him.

"Miller! Get to the LAV! They are coming for you!" yelled John, no doubt watching from the walls.

"We need to go!" yelled the Private as he kicked the door out of the rolled Humvee and dragged Miller out by his armpits. "Get up, sir!"

Miller got onto his hands and knees as he vomited on the ground in front of him. The Private was still dragging him away from the vehicle. He didn't understand. The other Humvee drove up next to them and the driver got out and started shooting his rifle.

"Get to the LAV!" yelled the other driver. Miller slowly stood up and turned around. He looked through the smoke of his wrecked truck and just 30 yards away, thousands of the infected were sprinting for them. "Our only hope is the LAV! Go!"

Miller turned and ran towards the armored vehicle with the 2 men on his flank. He wanted to go faster but he had cut his leg in the crash and it slowed him down.

"They are closing on us!" yelled one of the men who turned and shot at the swarm. "15 yards!"

Just ahead of them the ramp dropped on the LAV and one of the men inside ran out and fired at the swarm.

"Get the fuck in!" yelled the LAV soldier.

Miller could hear the swarm just behind them. They would have the group within seconds. In one last push, Miller dove and landed inside the LAV. He turned and looked as the other 3 men made it inside. The last man pressed the button to the door. It slowly closed just as the swarm got to them. As it sealed, all that was heard was the screeches of the beasts outside, their claws, and the rocking of the LAV.

"We are so fucked!" yelled one of the Privates in the vehicle. There were now 6 men in total inside, and all of them were terrified.

"Sir, what do we do?" asked a soldier to Miller. He didn't answer. "What do we do?"

—

John watched as Miller's Humvee rolled and flew through the air. He watched as the few men ran for cover and made it to the LAV, which was swarmed and disappeared under a mass of grey flesh.

"Miller are you still with us?" John asked, fearfully over the coms. After a few seconds he had an answer.

"I'm here. John. We are in some deep shit, man." Miller replied. "Did you get them off of the fences?"

"For the most part. They are still coming but you led the mass away." John replied.

"Good." Miller said, and paused. "John. I don't think I am getting out of this one. We are trapped. It's only a matter of time before they get in. I am sorry I brought this on you."

John paused, not knowing what to say. He didn't know how he could help.

"It's not your fault. You didn't do this. This isn't over." said John, reassuringly to Miller.

"It is over. I am sorry." said Miller. Before John could answer he heard the sound of a helicopter firing up and taking off.

"What the hell?" said John to himself, looking towards the tarmac. Into the air rose a black hawk helicopter. There was only one on base and only one man would be on it right now. "Hodge is making his escape."

NINETEEN

The sounds of fighting sounded all over the base as Hodge and his remaining men ran towards the tarmac, dragging the now infected LeBlanc with them. The beast that used to be his second in command snarled and threw his arms all around. Ahead of them, the chopper was started and ready to take off. The crew chief opened the side door and greeted him.

"Colonel Hodge. We are ready for take-off, sir." said the crew chief as Hodge boarded.

"Good, it's about time god damn it. Let's get the hell out of here!" yelled Hodge. The rest of his men loaded into the chopper. They shoved LeBlanc in and strapped him down to a seat. He snapped his jaws, which were beginning to grow pointed teeth, at the closest guard. The man jumped backwards in fright.

"Are you sure about bringing this along?" asked one of the soldiers, referencing LeBlanc.

"What are you going to do? Stay here?" asked Hodge, with an egotistical chuckle to himself. The man shuffled his feet but decided to get inside the helicopter. "Let's get the fuck out of here!"

The helicopter began to lift off of the pad. Hodge sat back and smiled at his successful plan. This was the new America in the new world. The time of the old ways was over and it was time for a new reign of power to begin. It was time for a new nation. A nation of The Chosen.

Over the past few years the terrorist organization (at least that's what the government had labelled it) known as, The Chosen, began to grow and find their strength. Hodge had always been partial to the ideals that the group preached, but did nothing. He stayed neutral against his better judgement. The nation was splitting as fighting picked up. Hodge always hated how the United States government did things and saw an opportunity to gain himself some power.

After the discovery of the first bridge made the public news, The Chosen had openly preached its link to the lord. They wanted it and they would do anything for it. Hodge saw his chance and reached out to The Chosen. He had tracked down the leader of the group and cut a deal. He would reveal the location of the facility holding the bridge, and in exchange he would become the second in command for The Chosen. This deal was immediately struck, and Facility 12's location was revealed. Hodge set this whole thing in play, he was the reason behind all of it. It had cost him his own grandson, but the trade would be worth it. He never imagined a new world like this. God was here and the infected were his disciples. The infection was the will of the lord and it was up to Hodge, through The Chosen, to spread it. Now that he understood it, he would work with The Chosen to use it to cleanse the world of the impure.

As the helicopter rose above Fort Hodge, he looked down and saw the fighting. Those poor fools, fighting something they didn't understand. It was a shame they all had to die, but it was the will of the lord after all. Hodge smiled grimly and kept thinking; but he was too far into thought to realize what was happening inside of the helicopter.

Across from Hodge, the infected LeBlanc had managed to wiggle and loosen the straps restraining him in the seat. He was able to work his head around and gnaw through the straps holding his arms down, and using his new strength, tore out of the restraints.

"Holy shit, kill it!" yelled one of Hodge's men as LeBlanc dove across the inside of the chopper and tore out another man's throat. It hung in his teeth as he whipped his head around and snarled. Another man pulled a pistol and fired at LeBlanc. A round hit the infected man in the hip, but it didn't slow the beast. LeBlanc dove onto his new target and began shredding the man's face with his newly forming claws. The man screamed in agony as the inside of the troop bay was splattered with blood. The man screamed and pulled the trigger on his pistol, wildly shooting. One of the rounds ricocheted off of the chopper's hull and hit the pilot in the back of the head. The helicopter began spinning, flying wildly through the sky as nobody was at its controls.

"No! This can't be! It wasn't supposed to happen like this!" yelled Hodge as the infected LeBlanc turned to him. Still strapped into his seat, Hodge was defenseless and LeBlanc began to gnaw on his calf muscle. The skin peeled off of the leg easily enough, revealing the meat below. Sensing the new food, LeBlanc began to bite chunk after chunk out of the screaming Hodge's leg, down to the bone. Hodge screamed but was helpless. He lived his last few moments in agony before the helicopter crashed to the ground and exploded, vaporizing everyone and everything within it.

—

John watched as the helicopter tumbled to the ground and exploded in the distance. He didn't know what happened with it. There didn't look to be any mechanical damage with it. All that John knew was that Hodge was now dead, and smiled.

"Hey buddy, there is good news. Hodge just went down in flames." John said to Miller over coms. He imagined Miller's smile at this news.

"Best thing I have heard all day." Miller replied. John could still hear the sorrow in his friend's voice, but there was a sense of grim satisfaction in the tone. The coms were silent until Miller spoke up again. "The clawing outside has stopped. What is going on?"

John, in confusion ran over and looked across the field at the LAV. The swarms of infected were distracted. They were looking towards the helicopter that had crashed further out. Before John could reply to Miller's question, the beasts started moving away from the LAV. Just then a radio transmission came over coms.

"Fort Hodge, this is command, over. Eye in the sky is seeing a massive draw away of the main horde towards that crash. I would use this time to prepare for the next wave, over."

"Roger, command." John replied and relayed the message to Miller. "Miller, if that LAV can still move I suggest you get that bucket of tin moving back here now. You are clear of hostiles for the moment."

"This ain't over yet. Headed back now. Get those gates ready because we will be bringing infected on our tail." said Miller, with a more hopeful tone.

John looked out across the field and saw the LAV was moving again. As it sped away from the crowd of cannibalistic beasts, it began firing its main cannon at the swarm, knocking down rows of them. Dirt kicked up behind the machine as it got closer and closer to the gates. A trio of men on the ground provided covering fire for the vehicle as it made it back into the base, keeping any stray infected from getting in behind it. Quickly, the gates shut and the crew of the LAV unloaded. John smiled and slapped a new magazine into his rifle.

"We are still in this."

<u>TWENTY</u>

Miller limped out of the vehicle as the gates to Fort Hodge slammed shut. He looked down at his leg and saw that the cut he received in the crash was still bleeding. It pained him to walk.

"Sir, that looks bad. We have a medic back in the command center that can patch that up." said one of the soldiers coming back from closing the gate.

"I'm fine." said Miller, gruffly as he stumbled across the blacktop of the vehicle bay.

"You barely survived out there, sir. We don't need you dying here now." said Edwards who was running down the stairs from the top of the wall. The man was worried about Miller, clearly, after seeing the mess that happened out in the field.

"Just worry about keeping this defense up. They let up now, but in a few minutes they will slam us again." Miller ordered, still stumbling out of the vehicle bay. The sounds of shots being fired echoed all around, but significantly less after distracting the main horde.

"We can handle this defense ourselves. You bought us some time, but you're no use to us dead, Miller." said a stern voice, crackling from yelling over gunfire. John.

"John, what are you doing over here? Those things will be hitting the east wall again at any moment." Miller said. After facing certain death, the man was all business.

"I got reinforcements over there after you drew the infected away. It's under control now. Miller, you need to go see a medic." John's tone was stern. "We've got this."

Miller didn't want to go. He felt that he needed to be here. He was the one that dragged these men into this situation after all; but John and the others were right.

"Fine. I'll go, but I want to stay in the loop with what is happening out here. If anything happens, I need to know." Miller said.

"You will, sir. I'll make sure of it. We all will!" said Edwards, eagerly. Miller nodded and headed towards the command center. As he hobbled away he heard shouts from the top of the wall again followed by the startup of more gun fire and mortars being launched.

"They are coming back! Keep the fire going, and get me a runner for ammunition!" yelled one of the men. The battle wasn't over yet.

—

"Rookie, I need you to keep laying down .50 fire on those fuckers. Don't let them get to the fence!" yelled John, but he knew there was no chance of stopping them from getting through. There were thousands of them and only about 35 men on this wall. They had all the firepower and lots of ammo to piss through, but they couldn't stop all of them. Unless help came soon, they would be pushed back into the buildings.

Rookie swept the M2 back and forth over the sea of grey out past the fences. The beasts reaching arms could be mistaken for the choppy waves of an ocean, and god knows there were enough of them to make it appear that way, too. The large caliber rounds that all of the mounted weapons on the walls and towers used were enough to blow a single beast into paste, but with this many, they didn't even seem to be making a dent. Across the horde of infection, the bridge still rippled, blue and glowing. Such a calming appearance for such a terrifying thing. Every time they thought the portal was done spitting out waves of creatures, more would start to come from it. They would die here. There was no mistaking it. The most they could do was pray and keep fighting back.

"I'm out!" yelled Rookie, shoving the gun aside and picking up an M249. The smaller, light machine gun wouldn't be as effective but it was something. The gun slammed back into his lean shoulder and he dumped spurts of bullets downfield towards the enemy.

"Where the hell is our runner?" cried Edwards as he, too, was nearing the end of his ammunition belt feeding into his M240. All across the wall, men were continuously firing. If no ammo came to them soon, they would be helpless. Lucky for them, the mortar fire was keeping up at a steady pace and the occasional rocket fired from a shoulder mounted LAW was enough to keep the establishing swarms in front of the fence in check. One group of at least 30 of the creatures began mounding in front of the first fence and were ignited by the flames as a

LAW rocket streamed away from the wall and collided with the group.

"Shit shit shit." said John as he unloaded a full magazine in full auto onto 5 infected diving towards the fence. He quickly dropped his magazine and slammed another one home.

"Runner! Here!" yelled Rookie as he spotted the man responsible for keeping the ammunition supply constantly coming. He wasn't doing a very good job, but then again, it had been almost 40 minutes of non-stop fighting and the man had to have been exhausted.

".50 caliber belts, here." said the runner, panting and speaking between breaths. He was sweating profusely. Rookie grabbed the belt and instantly began feeding it into the mounted M2 turret.

"What the fuck took you so long?" said Edwards, sharply, as he grabbed a box of 7.62 rounds for his M240. He fumbled with the belt in his shaking hands as he tried to pull it from the ammunition box. "God fucking damnit!"

"Relax, Edwards. You take his spot as runner and he will take over here. He can't take much more running" John said, calmly as he took 2 boxes of ammo from the runner and distributed the magazines within them to the troops around him. Edwards scoffed but got up and headed back towards the storage building as the other man replaced him, still panting. By now, Rookie was already back up and firing. The kid may have been new, but he was a good soldier and that is why he made it onto John's team.

As the battle continued, John looked to the first fence and saw that the creatures were massing in front of it, just as they had at the east wall. Their grey bodies, splattered here and there with the blood of their fallen comrades, piled against the metal chains. Some of them climbed over the crowd and attempted a jump over the top, only to be caught and skewered by the razor wire wrapped over it. They screeched and snapped their razor toothed jaws at the men firing at them from above on the concrete wall. As the mass built and built, the fence they piled onto began to give way.

"It's coming down!" yelled Rookie as he adjusted his fire towards the front of the pack. The massive gun boomed.

"They are building on the second fence now! We can't stop them!" yelled a soldier farther down the wall. The man yelled in a panicked voice and the rifle in his hands shook as he did, frightened by the flesh eaters getting closer.

The creatures again, piled up onto the second fence and like the first, it collapsed, letting the crowd onto the third and final fence before the concrete wall. The men above unleashed a storm of bullets into the horde. Just as the first few of the creatures made contact with the fence, the nervously shaking man from before stood up.

"We can't let them build up again!" he cried as he unclipped a grenade from his belt and pulled the pin from it.

"No! Don't!" cried John, but it was too late. The man threw the explosive out towards the front of the crowd. It fell short, clanking off of the top of the fence and thudded onto the ground just below it. The grenade then continued to detonate and send chunks of the metal fence flying all around. The fence around the explosion snapped and bent outward making an easy access hole. Dust and smoke blocked the line of sight to the new hole in the fence. Then, suddenly, several snarling beasts sprinted through the hole.

"They're through! Don't let them up the wall!" yelled a Sergeant to his men farther down the wall. Everyone paused their shooting and adjusted their aim to the immediate threat just below them now.

"Oh fuck this." cried the nervous man who threw the grenade. He dropped his rifle to the ground and ran down the stairs off of the wall. Once down from his position, he took off towards the command center. Seeing his brother in arms turn and run, another man dropped his rifle and also took off running behind him.

"Hold your ground! If they get through we are dead! We are all dead!" yelled John, grabbing another Private who had turned to run by the collar and threw him back to his position on the wall. The man looked at John scared, then nervously took his rifle in his hands and resumed fighting. Below the troops manning the wall, groups of flesh eaters began piling onto one another and climbing. Their razor sharp, rock hard claws latched onto the concrete, digging out tiny holes for grip as they pulled themselves upward. The sounds of scratching were heard over top of the screeches of the infected as they quickly maneuvered this obstacle ahead of them.

"They are right on top of us! Knock them down!" ordered John to the men as he angled his rifle vertical to the wall and fired down onto the beasts only a few feet below, now. The things were so close now that he could smell their stink of unwashed, weathered, skin and rotten breath.

"They're getting up! They're-" yelled a soldier as a grey, clawed hand reached over the top of the wall and grabbed him by his face. He screamed as he was dragged over the top of the concrete and thrown down into the sea of tearing teeth. Within seconds he was dismembered, below. Where the man previously stood, an infected man crawled over the wall and screamed towards the men next to it. Before it could make a move, a hole the size of a grapefruit was blasted into its side, revealing ribs and gore. The beast stepped backwards screaming and another hole appeared in its chest. John looked to his side and saw Rookie had left the stationary gun and was now holding his tactical shotgun, feeding more shells in to replace the ones he had just fired.

"Enemies in the wire. That turret is useless if they get behind me." Rookie stated as he turned and fired another round of buckshot into the face of another infected as it peeked over the wall in front of him. John nodded and kept up his fire. All around them on the wall, men screamed as they fought wildly or were thrown into the grey ocean below. He looked out and all he saw was the monstrous swarm, but just before he could accept defeat, a transmission came through his headset.

"Fort Hodge, this is Killer 1, over. Ready to lay down some fire for y'all below." said the voice with a southern drawl. John heard the chopping of propellers and looked up to the sky. Above them, an apache attack helicopter hovered above the wall. John smiled, reached up to tap his headset, and spoke.

"Bring the rain." he said as the 30 millimeter cannon on the helicopter began firing onto the horde, sending limbs and dirt flying. Rockets soared from the vehicle, detonating and igniting flames onto the plains. The advance was now being slowed to a manageable level by the men on the wall. This would buy them more time. John smirked, but it quickly faded as he heard another radio transmission come through.

"Be advised, eye in the sky is seeing several tengos slipping through defense on the west wall and headed towards the buildings, over."

—

Miller had his wound patched up and his leg was now wound with gauze and medical tape. He could walk but had a hell of a limp. Regardless of his leg slowing him down, he had been eager to get back to the fighting outside and left the command center. Walt had argued with him intensely about it, but Miller could hear the sounds of war outside. The explosions and screams drove the man nuts and he couldn't sit idle any longer. Miller had grabbed his rifle, packed his vest full of magazines, and hobbled outside to join the fight. Upon opening the door, all that he heard was shots all around him. Smoke rose from outside the walls and men were running position to position across the base. The screeches and growls of the horde outside were very audible. They were enough to strike fear into anyone, but Miller didn't care. In his mind, he had brought this upon these men and he would see to it that they would make it out alive. As he hobbled out into the quad, he saw a squad of 4 men rushing past him.

"Enemies in the wire, enemies in the wire. West wall, report!" yelled the Sergeant into his coms as he ran past. Miller reached out and snagged his arm, stopping him.

"What the hell is going on?" asked Miller. The man was in no mood for a discussion but stopped out of respect.

"Sir, we don't have time to talk. There are infected inside the walls. They broke through the west side. We are going to make sure it's secure." the man replied quickly, glancing off towards his men who were still running to the west wall. He looked terrified.

"Shit, I'm coming with you" Miller said, gruffly as he let go of the man's sleeve and pushed him along towards his men. The man stutter stepped, looking at Miller's bandaged leg.

"Sir, you- uh-" he kept glancing at Miller's leg and then shook his head. "Fuck it. Let's go. Try to keep up, sir. We can't waste any time."

Miller winced from the searing pain in his leg, and jogged after the squad, still with a serious limp. The group ran across the quad and past the barracks towards the west wall. For the first time since being at Fort Hodge, the barracks were empty. The only other people around were the occasional runners grabbing ammunition from the ammo storage next door. As the group got close to the west wall, they saw that the situation seemed to be already under control as several squads of men were atop the wall firing down at the small swarm of infected that had broken off from the main horde up front, and flanked them. Behind the wall and the men, bodies and gore laid all around the lawn. There had to have been 30 infected bodies lying around, and thankfully only a few dead soldiers. The Sergeant that Miller had followed had ordered his squad to check for wounded while he and Miller went up the wall to find out what had happened. Miller limped up the metal steps and found himself approaching a soldier with a massive gash across his back. The man fired a few shots from his M4 and turned to address Miller.

"Lieutenant, sir. We had a shit show on our hands over here." said the man, whose insignia showed that he was a first Sergeant, most likely the one in charge here. Behind him, blood dripped from his torn shirt. Had he had time to throw on his combat vest, this wound may have been less extreme, but like many others on the base, he was not ready for combat when the bridge opened outside.

"What happened here?" Miller quickly asked, looking around at the tired faces of the men on the wall.

"I think that I have a pretty good guess." the Sergeant with Miller said quietly, looking over the wall, horrified. Miller stepped over next to him and peered down. The fences outside of the wall had been toppled, leaving nothing from stopping the flanking swarm from getting up this wall that wasn't properly defended against such an attack. Before Miller could ask how this had happened with such a small swarm of infected, he found his answer. Against the base of the wall below, Miller spotted a massive beast. The thing had to have been the size of 4 men put together. It was covered in brown, patchy, almost mangy, fur, matted with blood. Its massive head had jaws large enough to almost rip a man in half. Judging by the blood around its face and the pile of innards mixed with camouflage fabric around it, it had. Luckily for them, however, the beast was now dead.

"Is that a-" Miller started, but his sentence was completed by the wounded first Sergeant in front of him.

"It's a goddamn monster bear. A big ass infected bear. The thing plowed through the fences like a goddamn battering ram and before we knew it, it had scaled the wall." the first Sergeant said not batting an eye away from it, the rage showing in his dark eyes. "First it just about bit my Corporal in half before anyone could react. Then it took a swipe at my back. You can see how that went for me. Luckily for me that thing hits like a bitch." the man said with a quick chuckle. He looked back down at it and spit. "Well, it learned that I don't." He lifted his rifle and showed his attached M203 grenade launcher. "Fired this bad girl point blank into its skull and it toppled back down."

"Holy shit." said Miller, amazed at the man's will to live.

"Yeah well that didn't stop the smaller bastards from getting inside the wire. They took out a quarter of my men before we beat them back." replied the wounded man, now pale from blood loss.

"You should go see a medic, soldier." Miller said to him, seeing the blood puddling behind him. The man looked at Miller's leg and smiled.

"All due respect, sir, but you're the last one to be saying that." he said. "I'm staying with my men."

"Fine. So what happened next?" Miller asked.

"Well about 3 of the little shits got through and took off towards the command center. I sent a hunter killer team of a few men after them but I haven't heard shit. Then y'all showed up." the wounded man replied, and then turned his attention back to the fight as he began shooting again. Miller quickly walked back down the steps and spoke into his coms.

"Walt, we have a situation." Miller said. No answer. "Walt! Answer me dammit!" Still, there was nothing. Miller charged his rifle and turned to the man he came here with. "I need your help."

"Yes sir." replied the soldier as he snapped to attention.

"Leave your men here to assist in the defense. You and I are going back to the command center. Something is off."

TWENTY ONE

"My name's Rollins, by the way." said the man jogging next to Miller as they looked for any sign of the hunter killer team on the way back to the command center. Miller ignored him. He was focused.

"I was right there not ten minutes ago. What the hell could have happened since then?" Miller said to himself. Had he stayed put like Walt suggested, they wouldn't be in this situation. They were almost at the entrance now and hadn't seen a thing.

"I'm sure that things are fine in the command center, sir." said Rollins, noticing the worry on Miller's face. Again, Miller ignored him. Rollins, still, kept trying to start a conversation. "So they can infect animals now? What's up with that?" Miller had enough.

"We have bigger things to deal with right now, than your name and what we have seen. You need to focus right now. If those things take our command, we have no communication to our extraction. You get that right?" said Miller, annoyed, to Rollins. Rollins went silent and put on his game face.

"Oh. Sorry." is all that he said. As the two men approached the entrance to the command center, they heard a man yelling for his life. They quickly entered the doorway and saw one of the creatures that they were hunting was on top of a struggling soldier. Miller quickly raised his rifle and fired a single shot into the beast's head, dropping it off the man. The man quickly shuffled his feet and pushed himself back against the wall behind him, which had streams of blood running off of it from another already dead soldier next to him.

"Holy shit, thank you so much!" cried the man, with his head in his hands.

"There are two more! Where did they go?" asked Miller, quickly.

"What? There are more! We are screwed!" cried the man, now shaking his head in his hands. "Game over! We are done for!" The man was panicking and putting no effort into helping Miller. Miller suddenly realized he knew this man, and the dead man next to him.

"Hey, you're from the main gate. You were with Staff Sergeant Rodriguez on the wall." Miller stated. The man looked up, dumbfounded.

"Yeah? I was." the man responded. Miller noticed that neither he nor the dead man had a weapon. Very strange for soldiers in an open warzone.

"What the hell are you doing down here? We didn't call for backup." Miller looked over the man and saw no wounds on him. Not even a spec of blood aside from the smear on his back from the wall. "You're not wounded. What are you doing here?"

"We-Well. We ran." the man said, breaking his eye contact with Miller in embarrassment.

"You ran? You were just going to leave the men there to die?" Miller asked, now angry with this soldier.

"They broke through, man! We couldn't stop them!" cried the man yet again, still not making eye contact. Miller glanced towards the north wall where this man came from. He saw the Apache helicopter hovering above as it fired streams of rockets down onto the horde.

"Yeah, it really looks like the wall is lost." Miller said, sarcastically. This man did not deserve to be saved. He read the man's name tag. Private First Class Able.

"Well, it was! They are crazy to stay there!" Able cried.

"Well I'll give you two choices, Able." Miller said. "Either I take you back to your position and toss you over that fucking wall myself, or you help us clear this building." Able looked distraught.

"You're going after those things? You're fucking crazy!" Able yelled, shifting his sitting position on the ground.

"So you're going over the wall then, you're saying?" Miller asked, firmly. Rollins sat back and watched the exchange in awe. Able shot up onto his feet quickly.

"Jesus Christ. No! I'll go, okay? Shit, man." Able said, seeing that Miller was not fucking around. Miller unholstered his Colt 1911, cocked it, and handed it to the man.

"Great, let's go." Miller said as he took point and moved further through the entrance down the hallway of the command center. Rollins continued after him, but stopped as he noticed Able waiting to take the rear of the group.

"Oh no. You're going to stay right in front of me where I can make sure you don't leave us." Rollins said to Able, motioning with his hand for Able to take his lead. Able sighed and followed Miller.

"You both are fucking crazy." Able said under his breath. Miller let the comment slide. There was a bigger priority than a mouthy deserter.

Miller quickly, but cautiously, walked down the hall to another double set of doors closed and marking the entrance to the main foyer. On these metal doors he saw what had to have been claw marks scratched across the middle from where the 2 creatures had pushed their way through. Miller, Rollins, and Able stacked up onto the doors in a breach and clear formation. Miller looked back to check that they were ready. Rollins nodded. Able was still shaking his head. Miller counted down on his fingers from 3 and then pushed through the doors, rifle up. Upon entering, he saw the place was a mess. Papers were thrown all over the place, chairs and tables were toppled. There was blood splattered on everything. Around the foyer there were no bullet casings or bullet holes, because aside from Walt and the soldier on the radio, Ackerman, the building was full of non-combatant support staff. Miller looked around the room as he patrolled the area and saw several of these support staff slumped lifelessly over railings or on the floor. Some were torn apart and fed on, others killed for sheer sport.

"Fuck." Miller said, seeing a headless woman who was hanging by her foot from the ceiling.

"You see! You see how fucking stupid this is!" yelled Able.

"Able, keep you're fucking voice down." Rollins said through his teeth.

"Fuck you! Look at this shit! You're crazy!" Able yelled again. He stomped over to a toppled computer monitor and kicked it across the floor.

"Able for the love of god, shut up and fall in line." Miller ordered, now nervously aiming around the room. This noise would attract the attention of the creatures and Miller knew from experience that being inside a building with 1 alone was risky, and here there were 2.

"God fucking dammit. I don't want to be here! I want to go! I can't take this!" Able cried as he stomped over to an open doorway.

"Able, shut up!" Miller hissed. Somewhere in the building, a creature screeched. Able turned and faced the other two men in the group.

"Why? What's the point? Who will be left to save? What we need to do is-" he started but before he could finish his thought, Miller noticed a tall shadow in the darkness of the doorway behind Able.

"Move!" yelled Rollins, too late. A pair of clawed, grey fleshed hands quickly reached out and grabbed both sides of Able's head and heaved him into the air.

"No!" screamed Able as he wildly fired the pistol in his hands around the room. One of the rounds whizzed past Miller's head and he ducked. The hands grabbing Able slammed his head hard against the top of the door frame and tore a gash in the side of the man's head, knocking his helmet off.

"Take it down!" yelled Miller to Rollins who was trying to line up a shot without hitting Able. He side-stepped around obstacles in the room trying to get an angle but couldn't.

"I don't want to die!" cried Able as his gun clicked, empty. The hands threw him to the ground with a loud thud and broken glass impaled the man's face as it whacked off of the tile floor. There was an audible crunch as his nose snapped. Able raised his mangled face from the tile and looked to Miller. He moaned.

"Die!" yelled Rollins as he fired his rifle into the doorway. Bullets pinged off of the metal frame. One of the rounds found a home inside the beast and he jerked backwards into the dark room. Rollins kept firing until his rifle was empty. Panting, he quickly grabbed a new magazine and slammed it into his gun.

"Rollins, cover me." Miller said as he crept forward towards the mangled mess of a man on the ground. Able moaned and spat blood onto the floor as it drooled off the end of his chin. He lifted one of his arms towards Miller. It was clearly broken as it was at an unnatural angle.

"Don't-let-it." Able moaned under his breath. He stopped talking and spoke one last time. "I'm sorry." Before Miller could grab the man, Able's legs were snatched in the doorway and he was whipped away, into the darkness of the room, screaming. His screams echoed as he got farther and farther away from Miller.

"Move!" Miller yelled to Rollins as the two men burst through the doorway and into the room, which appeared to be an office. Miller clicked on his rifle mounted flashlight and shined it around the room. A blood trail smeared across the floor from where Able was laying, into the office, up a wall, and into a ceiling vent. Miller still heard Able's screams echo out of the vent and go silent.

"Good lord." Rollins said, looking at the mess. He walked over the pool of blood where Able was attacked and picked up the man's helmet. He shook his head and handed it to Miller. Miller grabbed the helmet and looked at a photograph taped to the inside of Able surrounded by his wife and little boy. The writing on the photograph said "Philadelphia, 2019". Assuming this is where Able was from, it made sense why the man was in hysteria. Philadelphia was gone, and everyone in it. Miller set the helmet onto a desk and walked back into the foyer.

"What's the plan now, boss?" asked Rollins.

"We need to keep moving and find these things." Miller said, and moved forward down another hall.

—

"Yeah! Let them burn!" yelled Rookie over the sounds of shooting and explosions. Out across the valley the horde was being torn to bits by the attack helicopter above. The support had shown itself just in time and saved them.

"We might make it out of this thing alive!" yelled John, smiling. All across the wall, the men and women cheered while they continued firing onto the horde. The morale of the troops increased with this new support. All walls were secure. The only issue that they had now was that the command center had gone quiet. John hoped that everything was okay but there was a team dispatched to assist with that problem, and he tried not to worry.

"Look! We are beating them back, now!" yelled a woman to John's right who was firing vigorously. She was right. Now that they had support, the helicopter, wall fire, and mortars were making a significant dent in the assaulting wave.

"Killer 1 to Fort Hodge defense, we are low on ammunition and need to resupply." John's heart skipped a beat when he heard this, as it meant that the attack helicopter would be leaving, but was relieved when he heard what the UAV feed was showing.

"Fort Hodge, please be advised that enemy forces are decreasing. It looks like the bridge is closing." John heard over the coms. He looked out across the valley and saw that, sure enough, the glowing, shimmery, blue portal was growing darker. Suddenly it flashed, and disappeared.

"Hell yeah!" yelled a soldier near John as he saw this change in events.

"Let them have it! They have nowhere to go!" yelled John as he raised his rifle and fired a volley out across the valley floor. The thudding of the helicopter rotors became more distant as the vehicle flew away, and the sounds of shooting became more audible.

"We can end this, now!" yelled Edwards, who had just made it back with ammunition for Rookie's M2.

All across the fort, the beasts were being thinned out and men cheered.

"Kill them all! Kill them a-" John was yelling but stopped. The cheery look on his face disappeared.

"What's wrong?" asked Rookie. Then he too saw it.

Out across the valley floor, there was a bright blue flash and now 2 different bridges had opened up, one of them not very far from where the first gate stood, earlier.

"Oh no." Edwards said as he dropped the boxes of ammo he held out of shock.

The bridges rippled blue, just like the other, but no beasts sprinted out of them. No infected man nor animal. Instead there were swarms of lean grey worms, flowing out of the bridges in streams like water. They moved as one like a running river, over the mounds of bodies and through the scrapped, toppled fences. The soldiers on the wall fired down onto them but there were too many. They couldn't be stopped like the infected forms could. The worms made it to the base of the wall and began inching their way up it.

"We can't stay here. Everyone fall back!" yelled John as the first worms made it over the wall, overtaking several troops. Behind the flow of worms were the remaining infected, still numbering in the hundreds. The soldiers all grabbed whatever gear they could carry and moved off of the wall. Some leapt, not having time for stairs as the swarms were on their heels. If they could survive this, John would be amazed.

—

Miller and Rollins crept down the hall further. They were in the middle of the command center now and had found nothing but slain staff all around the building. The communication room was just up ahead and Miller hoped that Walt, at least, was okay. If Miller had stayed here, could he have stopped all of this? It was possible, but nobody here had expected the infected to make it inside the walls. Miller most likely would have been caught just as off guard and too, would have died. All he could do now was find any survivors and kill the infiltrator beasts.

"Did you hear that?" Rollins asked, snapping Miller back to the present situation.

"What?"

"I thought I heard something up ahead." Rollins said, nervously. Now Miller heard it. There was a dripping sound.

"Yeah, I hear it. It sounds like it's around the corner." Miller replied. He lifted his rifle and slowly peaked the corner. He saw blood pooling on the ground, with the slow drips of blood falling into it from above. "Shit."

"Is that Able?" Rollins asked.

"Oh yeah." Miller said. He looked up into the ceiling duct and saw the top half of Able's body hanging out. His arms were chewed down to the bone with little bits of flesh still left. His face was mangled and his jaw hung loose, cocked sideways. He would have been unrecognizable if it wasn't for Miller's 1911 still grasped in the man's right hand.

"That poor bastard." Rollins said, pulling his cross necklace from his chest and kissing it.

Miller approached the mangled carrion of a man and pulled his pistol from the stiffly gripping hand. He examined it, saw that it was still in good shape, slid a magazine into it and holstered it.

"The communication room is just ahead. We need to get there." Miller said and continued. Rollins followed, stopped at the body, looked up at it one last time, and again followed.

Miller could now see the metal door to the communication room, and the body that lay in front of it on the ground, torn open at the gut. It was the radio operator, Ackerman. Around him were bullet casings from his pistol and next to him was a dead infected.

"It looks like he managed to get one before he was killed." Rollins said, wide eyed at the scene in front of them.

Miller stepped over the corpse and looked at Rollins.

"You ready?" he said. Rollins nodded in approval and the two men pushed open the door.

Half expecting to see a bloodbath, Miller was relieved to see that Walt was okay. Inside of the communication room, Walt was standing with his arm in a sling, and a pistol aimed at the door. Behind him, two office staff cowered in fear.

"Holy shit, Miller. Thank god." Walt said, quickly lowering his gun. "These fucking things got in here and started to slaughter everyone. It was a bloodbath. We had no warning!"

"I know. I came as soon as I heard that they had broken through our lines." Miller said. "You okay?"

"Yeah, I'm fine. We heard screams and these two came running for help." he motioned towards the office workers. "One of those things got Ackerman and I locked us in here." He sadly glanced at the dead operator outside the door.

"There is still one in here, somewhere." Rollins said, peeking out into the hallway.

"It keeps coming back to us trying to get in. I think it killed everyone else in the building and wants us. It busted the bolt on the door last time it came. I thought you guys were it, again." Walt said, his voice shaking.

"Well we are here now." Miller said. "What's the situation outside?"

"Not good. They are falling back. I haven't been on the radio much to answer them. I've been a little preoccupied." Walt said.

"God damn." Rollins said. "We need to get back out there."

Just then, a loud screech was heard down the hallway followed by a banging in the vents.

"It's coming back." Walt said, stepping out into the hallway with Rollins.

"It's no longer safe here." Miller said to the two office workers. "Go to the tarmac. It's the safest place we have now. If help comes, you will be first on board." The two people nodded and ran down the hall towards the back exit. There was another screech closer now.

"It knows we are here." Rollins said. Miller now stepped out into the hall and raised his rifle. Above them, the beast clambered through the vents and screamed from the other side of the hall.

"It is trying to find a way to flank us." Walt said, shifting his aim to the left side of the hall.

"Back to back, now." Miller ordered. The 3 men now faced all directions, ready for the creature.

"We saw this one. It's big. Really big." Rollins stated, still looking through his ACOG sight towards the center hallway.

"3 halls and we are in the center of all of them. What luck." Walt said, with a halfhearted chuckle. The beast screeched and moved again through the vents in the center hall.

"Keep focused. It's going to come and come hard." Miller said. The men all grunted in acknowledgement. They listened to the sounds of the moving creature and then suddenly it went silent.

"Anyone have any idea where it is?" Rollins asked, nervously.

"Shit." Miller said. "I lost it."

"Same here." Walt said.

Just as the 3 men began to think that it had left them alone it burst from the vent in the center hall. Rollins was first to fire. The first round out of his rifle grazed the left leg of the beast, making it stumble, but it sprinted at the group faster than any of them had seen one move.

"Center hall!" yelled Rollins just before the beast shoulder checked him into the wall with an audible thud. Miller turned and fired at the thing, now right next to him. His burst landed into the right shoulder of it but didn't seem to slow it. It pulled back its massive, muscular arm and smacked Miller across the chest, sending him skidding across the floor.

"It's too fast!" yelled Walt as he fired his pistol into its back, while approaching it. Blood spurted from its front as bullets tore through it but it wasn't enough.

"Walt, no!" cried Miller as the beast spun fast and shoved its razor clawed hand up through Walt's stomach and out his back. He gasped for air as blood sprayed from his mouth and the beast lifted him into the air. Miller grabbed his rifle and fired at it, still laying on his back on the ground. Walt looked at Miller, shock in his face, and pulled his knife from his belt. Still held in the air, he stabbed at the massive arm shoved through him. The beast roared and flung Walt off of its arm and into the wall, with a wet slap.

"I didn't know it was this big!" yelled Rollins as he stood back up and fired again at the 7 foot creature. It reminded Miller of the one that had killed his family days ago, and he became full of rage. The rounds from Rollins and Miller's rifles punched holes into the torso of the beast but it didn't slow, still.

"Aim for its head!" Miller yelled as he got back up. The creature saw Miller recouping and kicked him in the chest, sending him flying into the communication room, slamming into the computer monitor.

"Die you big bastard!" yelled Rollins, just before the beast grabbed him and clamped down onto his neck. He screamed as it tore away his flesh and jugular. Its needle teeth sunk in again and took another chunk. It then swung Rollins' body like a baseball bat and smashed it against the wall, silencing his screams.

"No!" Miller cried as he limped out of the control room and drew his freshly re-obtained 1911. He fired several shots into the thing. It dropped to its knees, but then got back up. It hobbled over to Miller, towering over him. He aimed at its forehead and pulled the trigger. Click. The gun jammed. Miller frantically tried to pull the trigger again but the beast slapped the gun from his hand and heaved him into the air. It tightly squeezed all of the air from Miller's lungs as he stared desperately into its wide, red, bloodshot eyes. Miller grabbed Walt's knife that was still lodged in its arm and began to stab it just as Walt had. The beast screamed and slammed Miller against the wall. He gasped for air and dropped the knife. Now holding him against the wall, the beast opened its mouth, lined with rows of blood stained, serrated needle teeth. It reared back its head, preparing to bite down onto Miller, but before it could, a gunshot sounded from behind it. Blood sprayed from its skull onto Miller's face as a chunk of the creature's skull, blood, and black matted hair bursted away from it. The grip on Miller loosened and the beast slumped to the ground, dropping Miller. Miller sat up, panting for fresh air and looked over to Walt, who was slumped against the wall in a puddle of his own blood, smiling, holding Miller's rifle he had dropped. The barrel was smoking.

"Go save the others." Walt said, as he dropped the rifle to the floor in a clatter. His stomach was torn wide open. It was crazy he was still alive.

"Thank you, Walt. I'm so sorry for all of this." Miller said, now hobbling over to Walt. He picked up his rifle. Walt smiled back.

"It's okay. Go." he said as his eyes rolled back and he finally died. Miller looked away from Walt to Rollins' body, broken against the wall. These were just 2 more casualties that shouldn't have come to pass. Tears rolled down Miller's face.

Miller checked his ammunition, and began to limp away from the bodies and towards the door when he heard the radio crackle from the communication room. Miller had thought the device to be destroyed when he was kicked into there, but was wrong. As fast as he could, he limped back into the room and picked up the headset.

"Fort Hodge, respond. This is your final radio check." a voice on the other end said. The radio must have been receiving hails from Command while the men were preoccupied in their fight. Miller quickly put on the headset and responded.

"Here! This is Fort Hodge! We are here!" he said. There was a quick pause and the voice entered.

"Fort Hodge, this is Command. Your evacuation is arriving shortly."

TWENTY TWO

"Run! Get to the tarmac now!" John screamed to the groups of soldiers around him. He glanced back behind him and saw a flood of grey worms overflowing the top of the wall and onto the ground inside of the fort walls. All around him, men were running, occasionally stopping to take a few shots at the infected beasts that charged ahead of the sea of parasite worms, and turned to run again.

"Stay on your feet! Keep moving!" yelled Rookie, who stopped to quickly pick up a man who had tripped and was being trampled by the crowd of panicking soldiers. He heaved the man to his feet and continued running without a look back.

"Evac is here!" yelled Edwards as he whipped around and fired a burst into an infected man that had grabbed a straggling soldier by the collar of his shirt and whipped him back into the worms, screaming. Just ahead, approaching the tarmac was the first of the evacuation helicopters flying through the air. The chinook helicopter resembled a flying school bus as it hovered and slowly lowered itself down onto the landing pad below. The crew chief of the vehicle manned a mounted M240 on the ramp as 2 other marines ran down the ramp and began loading people on board. The first of the non-combatant staff were loaded and as quick as it came, the helicopter took off. John and his men made it to the tarmac and turned to form a defensive position.

"Oh no. They are coming at us too quickly. Far too quick." John said, as he looked around the base interior, wide eyed. Not far behind them, men were being overtaken by the worms. The slender creatures crawled up their feet and coated their bodies within seconds as the men screamed and flailed wildly, only to rise moments later as hungry, mindless beasts.

"What do we do, sir?" asked Edwards, who was starting to panic. He was breathing heavy and staring off into space. John looked around again. He saw a trio of soldiers in a sandbag bunker firing their machine guns into the swarm, only to be overtaken within seconds. One of the men had climbed onto the top of the bunker, only to be tackled off by one of the newly infected men who used to be his squad mate. John shook his head to focus, as another chinook began it's landing behind him. John looked around for anything that could buy them time.

"Those barrels of fuel! Over there! We can light a trail of fire!" John said, quickly. He pointed next to Edwards and Rookie towards 3 large, red, fuel containers. The two men quickly rolled the barrels out ahead of them one by one, plunging their knives into them to create a steady outward flow of the flammable liquid.

"It's done!" yelled Rookie as he and Edwards finished encircling the tarmac, and ran back to John. Men continued to flow to the tarmac, seeking the safety of the helicopters. The ocean of parasites were close behind, getting closer and closer. Next to John, Rookie popped the cap off of a flare and lit it. "Just give me the order, sir."

John looked out from the tarmac and still saw dozens of soldiers out there running towards them. If he lit the fuel, those men would be trapped on the outside, doomed to die.

"Sir?" Rookie asked, frantically. The flare trembled in his hand. A couple more men crossed the fuel line as John hesitated in giving the order. The parasites were only about 20 yards out now and closing. John looked behind him towards the landing pad as the second chinook took off with a load of staff and soldiers. Around the pad there were still about 30 men, desperate to survive. John looked back out to the 9 or so still running for their lives.

"Sergeant Rodriguez, we need to act now!" Edwards cried as he saw the horde closing in. The sea of worms was now coming from the left and right, as well as the front. 2 more men crossed the line while John pondered his order. The worms were now 10 yards out. He needed to act.

"Do it." John said, and a second later, Rookie tossed the flare onto the fuel trail and it ignited a ring of flames around the tarmac in a flash. Flames licked the sky in front of the 3 men as a third chopper landed behind them, too late for the 7 men stranded outside the ring of fire.

"No! Help us!" screamed one of the straggling soldiers, not visible through the wall of fire. His cries quickly turned to groans and garbles as he was overtaken by the worms. Many of the worms tried to squirm past the flames but erupted in a dull 'pop' as they were caught in the heat. The worms and infected quickly circled around the ring of flames and looked in on their prey.

"What have I done?" John said to himself in horror. One of the soldiers tried to run through the flames in desperation, only to become engulfed in them and fall to the ground, a burnt char. overhead, a black hawk hovered, its crew firing their mounted mini guns down onto the parasites. Aside it two AH-6 little bird helicopters hovered, firing their ordnance down onto the horde, as well. The beasts couldn't pass the fire ring and were being torn apart.

"If you didn't do that we would all be dead." Edwards said, wiping the sweat from his forehead. He was right, but the guilt would haunt John the rest of his life. Behind them, the rest of the soldiers all loaded onto the last helicopter. One of the marines from the chinook yelled after noticing John and his team standing there.

"Hey! This is the last bird out! We are leaving!" The marine yelled as he waved the 3 men to board. John saw this and motioned his men towards the vehicle. They ran up the ramp, joining the rest of the soldiers on board. John was the last on.

"Good to go! Lets get the fuck out of here!" yelled the crew chief as he fired the mounted M240 from the window as the helicopter lifted from the pad. They were safe. Below, John saw the base was swarming with grey shapes. Smoke from fires drifted through the air, and outside of the walls, the ground was littered with craters and bodies. John sat back in his seat and let out a long breath.

"I didn't think we were going to make it out." Rookie said, staring down at his shaking hands, coated with blood and grime. But they had. Somehow they had beaten the odds. They survived Facility 12, they survived the wrath of Colonel Hodge, and now they survived the assault on Fort Hodge. It was amazing, but they had done it.

"Has anyone seen Lieutenant Miller and Walt?" Edwards asked, quietly. The young man looked around the troop bay. "I haven't seen them anywhere." He was worried now. The question hit John like a rock. He had forgotten about the rest of his team, and had left them behind.

"Oh no. Jesus Christ. I am sure that they got out." John said reassuringly, mostly to himself. He peered out the window at the ravaged fort below.

"Forget that. Anyone who is not on a bird right now is dead." one of the other soldiers said, overhearing the conversation.

"There ain't no way anyone else made it out of that shit." the marine next to John said, also peering out the window. "A damn shame."

"You don't know that! You don't know Miller! He could have made it!" Edwards sobbed. Rookie patted his friend on the back and shook his head to himself. John had left his team behind. Not just his team, but his friends.

That was on him. Pots would be ashamed, he thought to himself as a tear ran down his cheek.

"It's done, kid. I'm sorry." said the marine to Edwards. Pity showed on his camouflage painted face before he looked away. The troop bay was now silent as all of the men relived the past events in their heads. Then the crew chief broke the silence, holding his headset to his ears.

"Hold up." the man said, and paused. "Holy shit. They are seeing some people still down there!"

—

Miller had been running for his life, or for lack of a better term, hobbling. His leg wound pained him and his ribs were broken, but he had to keep moving. Upon leaving the command center, Miller had entered hell. The defense had fallen and soldiers were running everywhere, trying to make it to the helicopters that had come to rescue them. Before Miller could make a dash for the final chopper, he was cut off by a sea of worms. Past the parasites he saw a wall of fire erupt around the tarmac and the chopper left.

"Shit. Not good." Miller said as he hobbled over to a storage shed to hide from the beasts that used to be his brothers in arms, now hunting the fort.

"Yo, over here!" said a soldier who bursted out of the shed's doorway. The young man scanned the area over with his M249 in an attempt to cover Miller, and he entered the shed, with the young soldier closing the door behind him. Inside the shed sat 2 more men. 1 was another young soldier, and the other was the wounded Sergeant from the west wall.

"Nice to see you again." said the Sergeant, gruffly. He was now paler than ever and his back was still not patched up, as his blood soaked through his clothing. "It looks like our brothers in arms have forsaken us."

"It appears that way." Miller said, peering out at the horde from between two boards of the shed. Smoke blew across the quad, making a fog cover for the army of creatures within it.

"We are fucked. We are so fucked." one of the young soldiers said, slapping his helmet with his hands.

"Stow your shit, Private. You're a professional, now act like one." the Sergeant said sternly.

"What are we going to do, sir?" the other young man asked, turning to Miller. Miller had no idea. As far as he had been concerned, this was finally the end for him.

"I-Well, I guess I don't know." Miller said, defeated. He was the most experienced man there was when it came to fighting the infected and now he was stumped. He had given up. The Sergeant laughed in the corner of the shed, quiet enough to not give away their hiding place to the infected.

"The man in charge with no answers." the Sergeant said, chuckling. Miller wanted to be offended but couldn't be. He was right.

"Ironic, isn't it." Miller said.

"Ironic? Man, you wanna hear some irony, get this." the Sergeant said, still laughing. "You know how I got wounded here?"

"A bear." Miller said, questioning the man's motives for conversing at a time like this.

"That's right. A big, fucking huge, infected bear. As if any of us knew that was even possible." the Sergeant stopped to laugh more and continued. "Did I ever tell you my name?"

Miller thought about it and realized he didn't know the man's name. He glanced down at the man's name badge. "Bear." Now it was Miller's turn to laugh.

"Born a Bear, killed by a bear. That's fucking irony right there." Bear said, smiling. He coughed and flecks of blood came up onto his lips, which he wiped away promptly. "See, most people would say what are the chances of that? I say that anything is possible."

"So what are you saying, sir?" asked one of the young soldiers, confused. Bear sat up in his seat and cleared his throat.

"What I'm saying is, anything is possible. We can sit here and wait to be torn apart by those things, or we can make a game plan and go down swinging." Bear replied. He was right and Miller knew it. With a sudden glimpse of hope, Miller stood up from his seat.

"What do we have for gear?" he asked. The men in the shed all looked down at their packs and vests and one of the Privates replied.

"About a half a box of ammo for my SAW, a few magazines between the 3 M4s, a frag, and a flare gun." the man said, shaking his head.

"Perfect." Miller said, now charging his rifle.

"Sir?" one of the soldiers asked in confusion.

"We are going to pop a flare for help, and if no help comes, we go down swinging." Bear said, finishing Miller's thought. The man had a big smile on his pale face. The Privates looked terrified.

"Do you want to die here as cowards, or try to make it out alive?" asked Miller to the men. After a couple moments they all stood up and loaded their weapons.

"Good." Miller said, confidently. "Make for the quad. With the tarmac cut off, that's the most open spot there is for a landing." The men all nodded. "We will succeed, gentlemen. In this life or the next."

Miller kicked open the door, stepped outside, and shot the flare gun into the air. The red poof of flame flew into the sky and slowly fell back to earth.

"Go!" yelled Bear, as he took off in a run towards the quad. He raised his rifle as he ran and fired a round into the skull of the nearest infected soldier, dropping it to the ground. The two younger men ran after him tailed by Miller.

Miller fired a burst from his rifle into a group of infected, dropping 2 of them where they stood. As the men shot, they drew the attention of the starving creatures and the parasites among them. Miller and the others made it to the quad and set up a defense between 2 decorative stone walls on the grass. The soldier with the SAW set up his bipod and opened fire onto the closest group to him, kneecapping them and forcing them to crawl.

"We can't hold them long!" yelled the other soldier who emptied his magazine into the torso of a large infected in front of him. The beast slammed to the ground in a puddle of blood. Before he could load his last magazine, a worm had managed to crawl onto his shoe and burrow itself into his ankle. The man screamed as the worm moved under his skin towards his spine. His skin bulged as the lean creature burrowed deeper. Before the soldier could turn into one of the beasts, Bear had popped a round into the man's head, killing him instantly. Bear turned and fired his M203 grenade launcher attached to his rifle into a swarm of worms, igniting the abominations in flames. Bear turned and fired more rounds into a swarm of infected forms just behind Miller, saving the man. Miller nodded, but before Bear could respond, he was tackled from the side by an infected soldier, who plunged his teeth into Bear's ribs. Bear screamed in pain but stabbed the beast with his knife, after pulling it from his belt. Before he could get into his feet, another infected man grabbed Bear and dragged him into a swarm of more creatures.

"You kill me? Hell no! Not today!" Bear pulled the pin on his frag grenade and held it to his chest. "Eat this you ugly bitches!" he yelled before erupting into an explosion, taking down 6 of the infected with him.

"Shit, I'm out!" yelled the remaining soldier as he dropped his SAW and backed up to Miller, who covered him.

Miller glanced down and noticed he was currently on his last magazine with roughly 2 shots left. He fired one into a diving creature, leaving it slumped over the wall where the other man just stood seconds ago.

"One left. I'm sorry." Miller said as he fired the final round into a swarm. The round hit but what happened next was unexpected. The swarm erupted into an explosion as a rocket streamed into them from the sky. A thudding of helicopter rotors was heard and a little bird zoomed past them, overhead, blasting the horde with its miniguns.

Miller stood in amazement, dropping his rifle to his feet. The little bird hovered above and fired more rockets and bullets into the charging hordes, as another one suddenly lowered down onto the quad just behind him. Miller snapped back to reality.

"Go! Get on!" Miller yelled to the other soldier, who quickly sprinted and hopped onto the side of the vehicle followed by Miller.

Miller heaved himself into his seat and held on for dear life as the helicopter lifted from the ground suddenly and zoomed away, just barely missing the grasping claws of the infected trailing them. He looked below and saw that they were only seconds away from being overtaken by the horde. He let out a deep breath of relief and looked to the young soldier to his right. The man was crying, staring off into space. He definitely was not okay but he at least was still alive. Miller looked to his left and saw the co-pilot of the helicopter handing him a headset. He quickly removed his helmet and put it on.

"Close call." said the co-pilot to Miller. The man's voice was monotone, unlike Miller, who was coming down from an adrenaline rush.

"Yeah, thank you so much. I thought we were done for." Miller said, panting.

"You're lucky, we were just headed out when we saw your flare and decided to make another pass." the co-pilot said. Miller took a few more breaths and spoke again.

"So where are we headed to?"

"General McCalister wants to meet you men, and find out what happened here. Especially now that New York has fallen." the co-pilot said.

"I saw the city fall. It was awful." Miller responded but was caught off guard by the next thing the co-pilot said.

"No, not the city. You don't know? You all were the last of the United States forces in the state. New York State has fallen. Anyone left behind is either dead or in hiding."

"The state? My god." Miller said, shocked.

"You all were on the last evacuation run. Anyone else left alive is on their own. With DC gone, McCalister is overseeing all operations on the east coast and is focusing on the defense of the southeast." the co-pilot said. Miller was silent.

The state was gone in a matter of days, soon to be the entire northeast. Miller sighed and clenched his fists in rage. The world was seeing the worst event in their history and it was his fault. He thought about this and remembered his personal mission. All he could do now was use his survival to help those who remained fighting. He would keep this world alive, and end the bridge events.

EPILOGUE

The sounds of gunshots rang out through the warm, Texas morning air. Samuel Hotch strolled down the walkway of the Texas capitol building. It was a beautiful day. The sun was shining high in the sky down onto the grass and trees around Hotch. He smiled as he took in a deep breath smelling the morning air, and thanked the lord for granting him such a wonderful start to his day. He continued down the walkway and strolled on past his soldiers who patrolled the area. Their bright red arm bands practically glowed in the morning sun.

"Good morning, brother." said Hotch, cheerfully, smiling from ear to ear.

"Morning sir! The lord blessed us today!" replied the young man, throwing up a quick salute to Hotch. This made Hotch even happier.

The squad of men continued down the pathway, most likely going towards the front gate to reinforce it. The men there had many issues trying to keep the peace with some of the more rowdy civilian populous outside of the capitol building. A real shame that people had to behave the way that they were; rioting and resisting orders of the troops. None of this would ruin Hotch's day, however. It was a good day and nothing could get in the way of it.

Hotch continued to the front steps of the building, which was guarded by 2 more men, armed to the teeth. The men stepped aside as Hotch moved past them, nodding and smiling. Before Hotch entered the building he glanced up at the flag banner waving in the breeze off of the top of the building. Its bright red coloring, marked with a black, rounded cross in the center stood out to the man. He closed his eyes, said a quick prayer to himself, and pushed open the double doors ahead of him, opening to a large lobby. The creak of the doors echoed through the room, followed by the thud of them closing. The sounds of shots outside were muffled now. Inside of the lobby, several of Hotch's men, all dressed in black with the exception of their bright red arm bands, stood at attention.

"Beautiful morning, ay boys?" Hotch asked the group, grinning. The men smiled back.

"Yes sir!" they all said at once. One of the men tossed a large rag to the ground in front of Hotch and he stopped to examine it. It was blue, white, red, and had stars on parts of it, where the bullet holes had not torn through it.

"You finally got that trash down from the top of the building, son?" Hotch asked the young man. The man smiled, showing his missing teeth through his patchy, black beard.

"You betcha, boss. I threw a better one up, too!" the man said,

"I saw! Its flying gloriously in the lord's light. Good job, brother." Hotch said, patting the man on the back. Before stepping away, he looked down and spat his chewing tobacco onto the rag through his bushy, white beard.

Hotch continued up the stairs, walking down the wide hallway. To his side, portraits were smashed and the walls were covered in filth and gore. His men had their fun. He walked around the corner of the hallway to another group of his men, this time with their guns to the backs of several enemies who were on their knees facing the wall. The enemies wore black suits, some in police uniforms, and others were merely civilians who refused to comply. These people were trouble makers and could prove to be a serious problem.

"Boys." Hotch said as a greeting to his men. The men still held their weapons facing the people on their knees, as they turned their heads and nodded.

"These are the last of them, sir. The building is secure." one of the soldiers said. Hotch chuckled aloud.

"Brilliant! Well then, as you were!" exclaimed Hotch, with a clap of his hands.

He walked away from the group as the men pulled their triggers, unloading entire magazines into the kneeling people. Hotch turned and watched as his men heaved the bodies and tossed them out of the window, onto the ground below. Hotch peered over the windowsill and saw the bloodied bodies piled up on top of the 20 or so bodies already laying in a pile down there. His men had done their jobs well.

Hotch strolled down the hallway till he came to a final door to a large office. Outside of it one of his men stood. The man saw Hotch approach and saluted, by throwing his fist to his chest. Hotch reciprocated the gesture.

"He is in here, sir. We have kept him locked in, alone." the trooper said.

"Good. Leave us." Hotch said, opening the door and stepping in. It closed behind him. Hotch was now in a large office, with a chubby, black man, behind a desk, shaking in fear.

"What have you done? What the hell is wrong with you people!" the man exclaimed. He had been crying for some time now, it appeared.

"Governor Jones! How are you? The lord has blessed us with a beautiful morning!" Hotch said with a big smile. He approached the desk and sat on the other side of it.

"The lord? The lord has forsaken us! Look what you are doing! Are you mad?" Jones cried, throwing his hands in the air. Hotch's smile quickly faded at this insult.

"Mad? Mad! How dare you! I am the chosen! I do the lord's will! How dare you!" he screamed, swiping the papers and vases off of the desk, shattering it against the wall. Jones jumped backwards in fear.

"You killed them, didn't you? My staff. The senators. All of them." Jones said quietly, not looking up from his feet. This was a silly question.

"Yes, of course. It was the will of the lord. They were sinners and needed to repent." Hotch said calmly. "I almost lost my head there, Jones. You have to watch what you say. Words can hurt a man." His smile now was back as sudden as it had left. Jones squirmed.

"What are you going to do with me?" Jones asked, now sobbing. Tears rolled down his dark skin and soaked into his dress shirt collar.

"Well, I have taken the city. Austin is now ours. Most of the state is in fact, ours. Your stronghold is lost. I would say you are out of a job." Hotch paused, looked at Jones in disgust, and continued. "Not that I fully understand how someone like you had this position to begin with. You are unclean and unholy. This is not the will of the lord."

"The will of the lord? You did all of this for what? You're fucked up beliefs? You racist, psychopathic, madman!" Jones yelled. The room went silent. Nobody spoke for several seconds. The only noises were the shots outside from the seized city. Then, slowly and confidently, Hotch pulled his revolver from his holster and aimed it at Jones.

"We are The Chosen and we speak for the lord." Hotch said, and then pulled the trigger. Jone's brains blew out of his head onto the wall behind him.

Upon the shot, the guard outside stepped into the room to check on the situation. He looked at the stained wall and smiled.

"Everything okay in here, sir?" he asked. Hotch smiled as he tossed the corpse out of the chair and sat down in the same seat. He kicked his legs up onto the desk, knocking dirt from his work boots onto the surface.

"Fine, brother. Everything is fine. Inform the men that Texas is now ours. The Chosen Land is now active." Hotch replied. The man smiled and left the room.

Hotch had founded his group of freedom fighters he called, The Chosen, years ago. He had led the group to grow and spread all across the United States over the years. Together, he and his new brothers had spread their god's will to the non-believers of this land, and cleansed the ones who stood in their way. It had been Hotch's mission to change this country of sinners into a new nation of believers; The Chosen Land. This was the start of his reign. His forces were spread throughout the Midwest. Kansas, Arkansas, and Oklahoma were full of his men, and now Texas was completely under his control. Nobody could stand in his way.

It wasn't long ago that he had received communication from a man from the United States Army named Colonel Hodge, claiming that he had wanted to join the cause. Hotch had been suspicious of this but had made a deal with the man, anyway. Hodge claimed that he had seen the gate to the holy realm, and that he could lead them to it. It wasn't long before he had proved himself to be a true ally to the cause. Just days after seeing these bridges on the news that the scientists in New York had created, Hodge had given Hotch the coordinates for the site of the research facility in exchange for being sworn in as second in command to The Chosen. Hotch promised that if this was found to be real, Hodge would have his wish. Hodge had given them details of the area, the defense, and anything else important. Hotch had tasked his closest follower with the task of seizing this facility, his own little brother. He knew this mission to be a suicide mission, but trusted nobody else to make communication to the holy realm, and his brother had succeeded in his mission. Although not what Hotch had expected to happen, these bridge events were devine proof that the holy realm existed. Whereas everyone else in the world saw these creatures from the realm as demons, he saw them as servants of the lord cleansing the world of its sinners. It was glorious. Most of these events had happened in the northeast, but some still happened elsewhere, giving Hotch a chance to see firsthand what the lord had willed upon the non-believers. Seeing another benefit of this, he also used the events as a distraction while he seized Texas. Minimal military was left in the state to defend against the coup, and what remained was now under his control.

Hotch now sat back in his chair, stuck a celebratory cigar in his mouth he had found in the desk in his new personal office and smiled. The shooting outside began to slow as The Chosen began taking full control. It was a good day. The best of days in fact. He was now the leader of a new nation that would change the world. Today, Texas was his, and soon, the world.